Where You Are From

Where

You

Are

From

Christopher Lee Nelson

REDHAWK
PUBLICATIONS

Where You Are From

Copyright © 2025 Christopher Lee Nelson

All rights reserved. No part of this publication may be reproduced, distributed, or transmitted in any form or by any means, including photocopying, recording, or other electronic or mechanical methods, without the prior written permission of the publisher, except in the case of brief quotations embodied in critical reviews and certain other noncommercial uses permitted by copyright law. For permission requests, write to the publisher, addressed "Attention: Permissions Coordinator," at the address below.

ISBN: 978-1-959346-80-7 (Paperback)

Library of Congress Control Number: 2024952252

Any references to historical events, real people, or real places are used fictitiously. Names, characters, and places are products of the author's imagination.

Interior Layout: Robert T Canipe
Cover Design: Erin Mann
Cover Image: Christopher Lee Nelson

Printed in the United States of America.

First printing 2025.

Redhawk Publications
The Catawba Valley Community College Press
2550 Hwy 70 SE
Hickory NC 28602
https://redhawkpublications.com

This work is dedicated to my mother, Karen McClough, whose steadfast belief in me defies reason; my grandparents, alive and passed, who taught me the old verities through their actions; and to Lenoir, my first tormentor.

"Say you were going on a trip knowing you wouldn't ever be coming back and all you'd ever have of that place you knew, that place where you'd always lived was what you could take with you. You'd want to think what to take along what would travel well what you'd really need and wouldn't need. I'm telling you, every day you're leaving a place you won't be coming back to ever. What are you going to leave behind? What are you taking with you? Don't run off and leave the best part of yourself. . . ."

—Jim Wayne Miller, from *The Brier Sermon*

Table of Contents

Footprint	11
No Better	23
The First Day It Felt Like Spring	39
Karissa's Weekend	57
What He Knows	65
Those Who Help Themselves	85
Even If	97
Strangers All	113
Where You Are From	127
Acknowledgments	137
About the Author	139

Footprint

"How much further?" I called ahead to Mitch, already a speck of motion on the horizon five minutes after our last break. I was exhausted. My thighs burned and my t-shirt was glued to my back by layers of sweat.

"What?" Mitch answered, turning around and peddling back to where I stood balancing my bike between my legs.

Mitch and I had once done this every weekend. One of us would call the other just after lunch – usually something our moms would let us make ourselves, a microwave pizza or peanut butter sandwich – and we would meet in his garage with our bikes, preparing to ride from our neighborhood into the wild of the Lord's Creek Rural Fire District. Those afternoons had been the highlight of my young existence. There was a certain freedom in taking to the road myself, riding a mile or two in the opposite direction from town into lands that didn't seem as familiar, as secure. But now, fourteen years old and about to start my first year at the high school, the whole thing didn't seem as fun.

"Where exactly are we?"

"Green Creek Road still. Though I'd say we only have about a mile or so more before we'll hit the intersection with Bottom Holler."

Mitch knew the area. I didn't. With the exception of a rare childhood car ride, I'd never been so deep into Lord's Creek before. My life revolved more around Tucker, the nearby town where my dad moved after the divorce and where I now spent my weekday afternoons sitting on his couch or shooting baskets at the neighborhood playground. Even before the divorce, though, my family had considered themselves to live more on the outskirts of town instead of the edge of Lord's Creek, and we'd generally avoided what my father still called "the hicks and the sticks."

Mitch, on the other hand, had never lived closer to Tucker than our neighborhood, where his family had moved when we were both five. Before then he'd lived in a trailer on his grandma's land out in this hilly wilderness.

That trailer was the reason we'd ridden so far. Mitch had gotten the idea that we should take a ride for old times' sake and, needing a destination, he'd come up with this. I'd agreed without thinking of how long a ride it would be, or about how out of shape I'd gotten since I'd started spending more time in town.

"You ready?" he asked, not bothering to hide his impatience.

I wasn't, but I agreed to ride on after Mitch promised we could take a break at the end of Green Creek.

§

Ten minutes later we reached the intersection with Bottom Holler, our road gently melting into the other in the middle of a curve.

It looked like we were heading into the backwoods. While Green Creek was a normal road by most people's standards – two lanes, smooth pavement, and brightly painted white and yellow lines – Bottom Holler was a deteriorating wreck. Potholes littered the narrow gray asphalt, bumpy anyway from the years that had passed since its last paving, and there weren't any lines, faded or otherwise, just a small, squiggly crack running down the middle to mark off the lanes.

"Which way?" I asked while Mitch stood by his bike, trying to light a cigarette.

"Up there. Hey man, you got a light?"

I dug around my pocket until I found my green mini-Bic and crumpled pack of Marlboro Lights. We'd just started smoking that summer after Mitch brought a stolen half-pack of his mother's Salem 100's over while my mom was at work. Being North Carolinians, we figured smoking was a necessary part of adulthood, and, being fourteen, we figured we were adult enough. I loved the feeling of rebellion I got watching the smoke twist its way from my mouth into nothingness, but I hated the minty taste of Mitch's Salems. They tasted too feminine, too weak for my idea of what a cigarette should be. So when I bought my first pack, I bought Marlboros. Cowboy killers.

I handed him the lighter after lighting my own. "How far again?"

"I'd guess twenty minutes, once we get going again. I just needed this before we got to Grandma's," he said, pointing at me with the cigarette.

While we smoked, I took my chance to glance around. Lord's Creek was right in the middle of what maps called the Brushy Mountain Range, a tiny ripple of foothills leading up to the nearby Blue Ridge, and its low peaks and shallow valleys surrounded us. It was a beautiful scene. A hawk circled high above a pine-covered hill, slowly spiraling its way down almost to the top of the tallest tree before beating its wings against the air and launching back up to start the whole thing again. I studied the black points of the bird's wings and the way that no matter how hard they pumped the tips remained pointed like arrows. I wanted wings like that, although maybe I just wanted to carry myself with that kind of dignity.

I almost pointed the hawk out to Mitch, but he was sitting Indian-style plucking dead grass up by the roots and lighting the ends with my lighter, lost in his own world. I watched as he stacked the singed blades into a pile between his legs, then picked them up and burnt them all again in one lump. It struck me that we were completely alone. I couldn't remember the last car that had passed, and there hadn't been a building of any kind for the last twenty minutes or so that we'd ridden on Green Creek. If something went wrong, there wouldn't be anybody to help.

Where You Are From

I stood to see if there were any signs of civilization on Bottom Holler or if Mitch and I had come to the edge of the known world. Across the street and down a couple hundred yards, two buildings sat in the flat bottom of the valley. One was a stubby, white-painted rectangle with an empty gravel parking lot. The sign out front read "Welcome to Lord's Creek Ruritan, Est. 1959" in hand-painted navy-blue letters. The other was an abandoned gas station. It was impossible to tell how long it'd sat there, but from the rusty scraps of metal leaning against the cinder block walls and the faded paint of the "Gulf" sign, which didn't even have the company's new logo, I guessed it had been a while.

"How did you live out this far for so long?" I asked, turning back to Mitch, who by now had stopped messing with my lighter and sat staring at the point where Bottom Holler disappeared over the lip of a hill.

"It wasn't bad, man." Then, after a minute of chewing on his lower lip he continued, "I loved it, to be honest."

"Why?"

"We could do what we wanted. Dad used to take me shooting up behind the trailer. We'd walk fifty yards, maybe less, and we could just shoot shotguns, rifles, anything. No worries about hitting anybody or the sheriff getting called. It was nice." Mitch never stopped watching the road while he talked, even when he stubbed the butt of his cigarette against a rock by his foot.

"What are you looking at?" I asked.

"Nothing," he said, turning around and pointing down to the Ruritan. "See that gas station there? When I was a kid, my mom would drive me down there on Saturdays if I'd been good that week and let me pick out any kind of candy I wanted. They had everything, things you can't find in town: Sugar Daddies, the big kind, not those little twigs they sell in the grocery stores; candy cigarettes; huge gumballs the size of your fist; everything. I thought I was in heaven." He closed his eyes and smiled, his chest expanding with a deep breath.

"When did it close?"

"A year or so after we moved. We drive by it every time we come out to see Grandma, but I've never really thought about it until now. I miss that place." Mitch sighed and got up, ending the conversation by grabbing his bike and starting off up the hill.

§

Bottom Holler was more fun to ride on than I'd thought it would be. The asymmetric vibration of rough pavement lulled me, and I opened my mouth a slit to feel my teeth chatter together. The wind picked up as we rode, and I felt my skin shrinking as the sweat dried, leaving only a film and a cool sensation.

"We're not far from Grandma's," Mitch called over his shoulder after we'd rode about a mile.

I looked for a house once I had crested the next hill, but all I could see was a forest of maples and poplars stretching to the next rise across both sides of the road.

"Over this hill?"

"Yeah, they're set back from the road." Mitch had stopped at the bottom, and I pulled up beside him, standing with my bike's crossbar resting against my thigh so it wouldn't fall.

"One more cigarette?" Mitch asked, holding the wrinkled green pack out with a shaky hand. I declined, pulling a Marlboro from its crisp box.

"I can't wait for you to see our old place. Nobody's lived there since we moved out. Grandma just uses it for storage and stuff, but we can still go in. It's in good shape." He told me all about the trailer while we smoked, about the nooks he'd used as hiding places before he got too big to fit in them, about the stains that were still on the walls from where he'd discovered a permanent marker when he was two. The longer he talked, the more excited he got, chattering away like a kid waiting in line at an amusement park.

"Can't wait," I said as I threw down my cigarette's butt and drug the heel of my shoe across it.

"Well, you ready to go?" Mitch pulled a pack of Big Red gum from his pocket, popping two sticks into his mouth and handing two to me. "For the breath," he smiled.

§

A few hundred yards down the road, a gap made of two tire ruts and a dented mailbox covered in ancient, dark brown rust appeared in the tree line. Looking up the ruts, which I guessed was the driveway, I couldn't see a trailer or house, just a tunnel leading to the right through a thick canopy of trees.

"This it?" I asked Mitch, who stood beside me at the tunnel's opening.

"Yep, just around that curve."

His grandmother's house was as I'd pictured it, a one-story shotgun shack with chipping white paint that revealed the graying, untreated wood beneath. A ratty, floral upholstered couch sat beside an old refrigerator on the porch. The house sat in a little square clearing surrounded by forest on all sides. The driveway ran through the middle, cutting two scars through the knee-high grass. The house was to the right of the driveway. To the left was an empty patch of red clay.

"I don't understand." Mitch stood beside where he'd dropped his bike, his hands at his sides. From behind, I watched his head swivel between the house and the bare ground.

"What's wrong?"

"Where is it?" Mitch didn't seem to be talking to me, but to himself. His voice cracked.

"Man, what's going on?"

Mitch slowly started walking over to the barren clay, leaving his bike lying on its side in the ruts' grass median. He moved deliberately, measuring each step like he was walking into a minefield. "My trailer, it used to be right here." He turned to face me and I saw he was crying. His eyes were swollen with tears, magnifying the brown of his irises so much that I stared into two dark circles.

"It's okay, man. Really." I didn't know whether things were fine or not, but said so because it seemed like something I should say. Mitch didn't respond. Instead, he sat down in the grass at the edge of the rectangle and rested his face in his hands.

"Hello? Someone out there?" An old woman appeared on the porch while I stood behind Mitch, staring over his shoulder at the trailer's footprint and wondering what I'd missed.

"Grandma, where's the trailer?"

Mitch wailed without standing or even turning in his grandmother's direction. I stepped over to the left, back towards the bikes, so I wouldn't be between them. It didn't feel like I was in the way, but more like I was about to see something I shouldn't.

"Mitch, is that you?"

The woman didn't leave the porch but moved to the bottom step, holding onto a wooden column for support. Thin flaps of skin hung limply from her arms and chin, and it was obvious that in her youth she'd been much larger. Her entire appearance seemed withered, and I got the impression that what I saw was a raisin where before there'd been a plump grape.

"It's me, Grandma." Mitch wiped his eyes and walked towards the house. When he got next to his grandmother, the difference in their size became apparent. While Mitch wasn't much bigger around, the elderly woman's permed hair barely tickled the bottom of his chin. "This is my friend Will," Mitch said, nodding in my direction.

Where You Are From

"It's nice to meet you, ma'am." I called loudly, even though I wasn't that far away. "Nice to meet you, too, young man," she yelled back, mimicking my volume perfectly in a scratchy voice.

"Grandma. What happened to the trailer?"

She looked across the yard at the patch of dirt and scrunched her face. I recognized the expression as one Mitch used. "You mean your old trailer?"

"It was here the last time we came out for Sunday dinner. Where is it?" Mitch paced back and forth in front of the porch while he spoke.

"They just came and got it the other day. Wednesday, I think. Doesn't the yard look nice without that eyesore? Your Uncle Curt's supposed to come out and re-seed that dead spot next week and mow the grass." She talked like it was a good thing, oblivious to Mitch's increased pacing or his muttering under his breath. "Cut them old plumbing pipes away, too," she said, pointing at a corner where two shafts of lead rose from the ground like relics of a people long dead.

"Who came and got it? What happened to all the stuff inside?" Mitch asked.

"Why, the men from the disposal company, I guess. Didn't your father tell you? He knew about it." She took a step forward, her arm hesitantly raised.

"No, he didn't tell me!" he screamed. "How could you do this?"

He ran across the yard to the bald spot, sitting square in the middle. "This was my home, Grandma. I grew up here. Doesn't that mean anything?" He choked on the words as he started crying again. I watched from my place in the yard, wanting to leave more than anything. But if I left it would draw attention to the fact that I'd witnessed as much as I did, so I stayed put.

Mitch's grandmother walked over and put her wrinkled hand on his shoulder. "Honey, I thought you knew. I haven't kept anything important in that trailer in years, and your father thought it was a good idea." Her voice was soothing. When she spoke softly, the scratch in her voice became a comforting defect, like the hiss and pop of my dad's vinyl records.

"But I was going to show Will my room," Mitch said, and they both looked in my direction. I tried to smile, but smiling made me feel like I was making light of the situation, so I just looked at the grass under my feet. When I checked they were still staring. Mitch was leaning his head against the hem of his grandmother's skirt. The sun reflected off his tears, making his cheeks shine.

"It's okay, man, really," I said for the second time.

"No, it's not!"

Mitch leapt up and ran across the yard, stopping right in front of me and poking his finger into my chest as he spoke. "You don't understand. I grew up out here, not you."

Mitch's grandmother slowly moved our way, calling to him in her best lullaby voice, "Mitch, honey, your friend's right. Things change, and I just couldn't keep the trailer up anymore. If I hadn't let them take it away, it would've fallen on its own."

But Mitch didn't pay her any attention.

"Gone. Never coming back." His eyes glazed over, and for the first time I felt a spark of fear. I'd never seen him like this before, out of control like an animal fighting off a too-weak tranquilizer. "Nothing left. There's nothing fucking left!"

"Come on, man, calm down," I said, holding the palms of my hands out and backing away. "I didn't know it was this important to you."

Mitch tore away from me and grabbed his bike, hopping on at a run and peddling down the driveway and around the corner out of sight. His grandmother called after him for a minute before turning to me.

"Poor boy. He's just upset," she said, pulling a knit shawl tighter around her chest.

I stood beside my bike, trying to think of something to say that would cut through the uncomfortable cloud that had settled over the clearing. I wished I could go inside with the old woman, maybe sit down with a glass of iced tea and listen to her tell a story or two, but without Mitch I knew it wasn't going to happen.

"I guess I'd better go. He might need me," I finally said. "It was nice to meet you, ma'am."

She didn't say anything back. When I glanced over my shoulder on the way down the driveway, she was creeping back to the porch, her head slowly wagging back and forth.

§

I saw Mitch's bike from the top of the hill overlooking the beginning of Green Creek Road. It was leaning against the back of the Ruritan, the bright green of its frame escaping from behind some abandoned boards stacked against the wall and forgotten. The parking lot was still empty.

Across the road, a thin column of smoke rose from the gas station. A sick feeling crept into my stomach, and I hid my bike in the runoff ditch beside the road, hoping I was wrong.

After a minute, Mitch appeared from inside the building. The column of smoke was growing thicker, a pale gray fog billowing from the broken windows. I watched him walk to the road and pause, looking up at the ridge I rested on. I closed my eyes and tried to disappear, to transport myself away from Lord's Creek and lost trailers and Mitch, but when I opened my eyes again, he was still there. For the first time all day I felt cold, and a shiver that started in my head passed through my body and into the ground beneath.

Eventually Mitch walked across the road and freed his bike from behind the Ruritan, looking both ways before peddling down Green Creek Road.

I waited until he was well out of sight before getting my bike from the ditch and pushing off down the hill. By the time I reached the turn, flames were visible through the windows, orange fingers shooting a choking cloud from their tips, and I could smell the burning decay in the air.

    I stood watching for a minute as the smoke coated the valley, then turned onto Green Creek Road and peddled as fast as I could in the direction of town, of home.

No Better

From her seat in the third row, Theresa can just see over the cheerleaders and Killdary bench as Mark takes another snap and drops back, his helmet swiveling like a machine gun spraying bullets before his arm jerks forward, the ball making a slightly wobbly arc – almost ghostly under the high-powered stadium lights – on its way to Jackson Fergusson at the South Wilkes twenty-five-yard line. The loudspeaker mounted above the scoreboard drones the words *first down*, stretching the *ow* into a howl, and Theresa screams along until her voice catches. It's the beginning of October and the chill bothers her throat.

It's shaping up to be Mark's best game of the season. By the late third quarter he's completed nine of eleven passes for a hundred sixteen yards and two touchdowns, and he's run the ball for sixty-four and another score. Theresa can tell that it is one of those nights when he's caught fire, that nothing will be able to stop him. And she still gets a thrill every time his name is announced over the loudspeaker, echoing off the tall concrete home stands and across the visitors' bleachers, even after being his girlfriend for the past six months, even after hearing it every Friday night since school started.

Two plays later, Killdary scores again, this time on a handoff to George Newman, right as time runs out in the quarter. The scoreboard's siren screams, and the band plays the fight song while Mark trots off the field, removing his helmet and staring straight at her until he's sure she's seen him

"He is so into you." Candice nudges Theresa with an elbow before pointing with her chin at the two rows of cheerleaders arranged on the asphalt track separating field from stands. "You know they're jealous."

Theresa doesn't respond. She barely knows Candice, another member of the club of players' girlfriends she's been initiated into without exactly knowing when or how. After the first couple games, when it became obvious that she was more than just a passing phase for Mark, she'd found herself no longer sitting alone in the top corner of the stands, but right smack in the middle, surrounded by them. But she's happy for the company, the authority their acceptance lends her.

Because it had been hard at first knowing that some of the other girls, mostly cheerleaders and daddies' princesses, wondered what Mark Spainhour – *the* Mark Spainhour from Saturday's sports page – saw in a country girl from Lord's Creek. She knows they assumed she was a slut because she isn't anorexic, isn't bottle-blond pretty, but she also knows that she doesn't do anything with Mark that they wouldn't. But enclosed within a group, she sees now that as long as she has Mark it doesn't matter. She's the queen of the game if nothing else.

"Is there anything going on after this?" Candice asks.

"I'll have to talk to Mark," she answers, keeping her eyes on the bench. She'd never been a big fan of football before Mark, and she still finds it hard to pay attention when he isn't on the field. She's far more interested in watching him on the bench, his hair spiked with sweat as he huddles by the coolers with his receivers, talking them through whatever plays they might run when it's their turn with the ball again.

"I thought I heard something about a party at the Banks'. I think Brian got his hands on a keg …"

Candice keeps relating all the gossip, but Theresa half hears her. South Wilkes gets a first down and calls a timeout, but they're more than three touchdowns behind. Mark is standing on the edge of the sideline watching the game with his arms crossed, his back to her. She half-wishes it was the beginning of the season again, when it wasn't getting dark until about this time in the game and she could see further than the clusters of spotlights on top of the light poles when nothing much was happening. The stadium is the highest point on campus, built into the foot of Killdary Mountain behind the school, and from the top of the stands she would stare across the roof and the flat creek bed that hides Upper Creek beneath a canopy of trees to the hills of Lord's Creek where she lives and the mountains that rise beyond. Another hill borders the school to the left, a shadow blocking out the dots of light from Tucker's streetlamps, but she knows they're there. They're there with Hopewell Memorial Hospital and her grandmother propped carefully upright by the nurses in their shapeless blue outfits that look like paper.

Someone passes on their way up the stairs, a friend of Mark's or at least someone who knows his name, and congratulates her on how well he's playing. While there's a twitch of bitterness at the interruption, she loves the recognition too much to do anything other than smile distractedly. South Wilkes had to punt and Mark is running back on the field.

"That was Jeremy Floyd," Candice says, watching him as he disappears into the crowd at the top of the stands. "He was the quarterback two years ago when we made the playoffs."

Theresa grunts. She vaguely remembers him now, a strutting figure who'd enlisted in the Marines after no colleges offered him any money for scholarships. Not like her Mark, who already has offers from two Division II schools but is waiting on either Blue Ridge State or Western Carolina. She wonders briefly what Jeremy is doing home, if he's on leave or got kicked out or what, but then Mark breaks through a hole in the South Wilkes defense again and she's on her feet calling his name, hoping he isn't lying when he says he can hear her above all the other noises out there.

"I'm sorry about your grandma," Candice says once things have quieted down and Killdary is once again patiently running out the clock. "Jeff told me she was in the hospital."

Theresa cringes. This is her escape. She manages to nod, say a quick thank you in the hopes that the subject gets dropped. She wonders how much more they know about her, if they know about her mother.

"Do they know what's wrong?"

"They think it's something to do with her arteries, but they're not sure yet."

"Is she going to be okay?"

The game is almost over. South Wilkes is out of time outs, and now all that's left is for Mark to kneel down once or twice before Theresa can go to him.

"I don't know," Theresa says, already buttoning her jacket in preparation for the wind she knows is blowing across the field.

"You can stay here if you'd rather," Mark says later.

They're sitting in his basement, though it's closer to a mother-in-law apartment than a traditional basement. Mark's parents had it renovated when he got to high school, complete with carpeting and a full bathroom, just so he'd have a place to hang out with his friends. It's nice, nicer than her living room, and when she's here alone with Mark she likes to pretend that it is her Home. Hers and Mark's.

"In your basement?" Theresa laughs. She's still a little giddy from the joint they'd smoked on the way over from the party, and she's pretty sure there's still some of Bates' beer swirling around inside her brain, too.

"Why not? My folks wouldn't care. I'd just tell them you weren't feeling well enough to go home."

Mark's sentences have the same staccato swagger he shows on the football field, and she allows herself to imagine curling up with him on the fold-out couch, his thick arms wrapping around her shoulders, better than any blanket. That's the only thing she feels has been denied to her in their relationship, the comfortable intimacy of a full night's sleep beside her lover.

"Where would you sleep?" she asks.

Mark falls backwards against the arm of the couch, pulling her with him so they face each other. His cheek was scratched during the game, a pattern of four thin red lines tying his right eye to the corner of his mouth. A South Wilkes cornerback had taken advantage of the confusion at the bottom of a pile. Theresa likes them. They offset the boyish effect of the dimple in his chin, a little pit too cute to be called a cleft, and match the color of his eyes, a shade of gray that mimics polished steel. To wake up staring into those eyes, she thinks. To put off dreading tomorrow morning that much longer.

"Not where I'd want to," he says, burying his face in the crook of her neck. "Mom may be cool, but she's not that cool."

It's hard to pull herself away from the fantasy, to surrender the warm bed she clings to in imagination. But she knows it's unavoidable. This is not a home they've made together. Mark will sleep upstairs in his bedroom across the hall from his parents. She'll sleep at home in the house her mother had grown up in, and tomorrow she has to get herself to the hospital.

"Then I need to go home," she says, breaking their embrace. She can feel the high dissipating, leaving her flat and vacant like the beach at low tide.

"Are you sure? I don't want you to have to be alone tonight."

She tries to smile. "That's going to happen whether I stay here or not; you said so yourself," she says, secretly happy at the sudden softening of his eyes. "Besides, Helen won't be awake when I get there."

She's told him all about her mother, about her fits, about what the doctors at the Health Department called manic depression, then bipolarism as the years went by. She's told him about her fears and hurts, and he's always been so supportive, so wonderfully protective. But what she hasn't told him is how used to it she is, like living with only one arm. A body learns to adapt.

Where You Are From

Once they're out of town and speeding down the Wilkesboro Highway she leans her head against the truck's door, exhausted. The angles of Mark's face stand out even more in the muted glow from the dashboard, a pattern of light and shadow that blends with the darkness outside. She wants to thank him, but she doesn't know how to without sounding pathetic.

The house looks deserted when Mark's headlights sweep across it on their way up the drive. It's not that the house looks any different than she'd expected – the tall weeds and loose siding are nearly permanent fixtures, and she hadn't expected Helen to leave the porch light on for her – but it feels different. There's a stillness, as if the air around the house had been drained of its oxygen. It's even worse after she's out of the car, walking through the twin beams of light in the night's dampness away from Mark, who waits until she's closed the front door behind her before the growl of rubber on gravel recedes back towards the highway.

The stillness is still there the next morning. The orange light filtering through the blinds in the living room makes the room look shabby and faintly sick as Theresa walks through on the way to the kitchen. She pauses for a minute, but the room is the same as it was yesterday and every day before that she can remember. The same mismatched furniture – a pink floral-patterned couch that was once dark red, the black cherry rocker, the end table with the TV balanced on top – the same scuffed hardwood on the floor, the same stained blinds hiding the casement window beside the front door.

Still, other than the noises she makes getting her mug down from its hook by the sink, the house is too quiet. The refrigerator hums for a few seconds every so often only to click off again, and the coffeepot that had belonged once to her grandfather pops and gargles the water she'd poured in. But nothing from Helen's room. Normally Me-Maw would be awake first, the sounds of her morning routine – her rattling dishes and soft mutterings – echoing through the house. It's Me-Maw who wakes Helen in the mornings. It's Me-Maw who makes sure she's taken her medicine.

Theresa glances through the window above the kitchen sink, staring down the twin ruts of the driveway until they veer left and disappear behind a gray shade of trunks and underbrush. Above the top of the treeline, the nearest of the Brushy Mountains forms a brown-gray bell of a horizon. It's the same view Me-Maw used to lift her up to see. The county is talking about letting the country club build houses on top of that ridge, though, and Theresa tries to imagine how different the picture would be with little toy houses looking down on them.

The coffeepot finishes, and she pours herself a mug. She needs to wake up Helen and get her bearings for the rest of the morning.

"Mama?" Theresa knocks again before opening the door. The silence isn't a good sign.

"Go away." Helen is little more than a lump in the bed hidden beneath layers of sheets and blankets, a few strands of pale hair the color of wilted cornstalks across a pillow.

"Damnit, Mama. You've got to get up." Theresa begins to pick her way across the floor. Stacks of books are piled up on the boxes Helen has scattered across the room. It's all the clutter that probably makes the light in this room seem cloudier than the others, a deeper hue of yellow more clogged with dust and stale air. Sometimes Theresa wonders if her mother's problem is connected, that the junk in her room somehow clogs up her emotions.

She reaches the edge of the bed and sits, her hand probing for the mound that contains her mother's shoulder. "Me-Maw's in the hospital, remember?" she asks, consciously aware not to take the wrong tone. She needs to sound nice without giving Helen the idea she's being patronized, a task that's harder than it appears.

Helen's head emerges, the green of her eyes locking onto Theresa. "I know. I'm the one who had to take her."

Theresa knows she shouldn't, but before she can help herself, she reminds Helen that she'd wanted to drive her in on Thursday and couldn't yesterday because of school.

"You little smart-ass," Helen snaps, throwing the covers off and sitting so that her back is to Theresa. "It's not like we can afford to just run to the hospital every time one of us doesn't feel well."

Theresa stands, afraid to lose any more ground. "Well, get dressed. I'll be waiting in the living room," she says on her way out.

A full fifteen minutes later, Helen appears wearing sweatpants held on solely by the tied drawstring in front and an old t-shirt with the words *Myrtle Beach* airbrushed in pink and black cursive across the front. Unlike most patients, Helen had withered with the changing combinations of mood stabilizers, her already skinny body losing flesh faster than if the doctors had taken to her with a filet knife.

"I'm not going," she announces from the edge of the living room.

Theresa looks up from where she stands in the kitchen – hovering over the pill bottles stacked neatly against the wall by the new cordless phone – then keeps searching. It's impossible to tell the difference between Helen and her grandmother's medicines just from looking, and half the bottles are empty, anyway, so she's been reading each label individually in her hunt for the full bottle of Seroquel.

"Yes, you are," she says.

"I'm *your* mother, remember? And I just don't feel up to it today." Helen comes into the room and sits on the couch, squinting at the windows like they're spotlights in a police interrogation. "They're probably busy running their tests and such, anyway."

Theresa's eyes drift back to the phone, wishing she could call Me-Maw for help, but a hospital room isn't somewhere you can just call for advice.

"Have you been taking your meds?" she asks, though she knows the answer. The medication makes Helen almost normal, a little dazed and shaky maybe, but functional. Without them she's a wildcard.

Helen pulls a cigarette out and lights it. "What, are you my nurse now?" she asks, the irritation in her voice vanishing, replaced by the first hints of anger.

"I'm just asking." Theresa pours herself the last cup of coffee and keeps looking through the bottles until she finally finds the right one, sitting slightly apart from the others behind a large bottle of generic ibuprofen.

"Well don't fucking ask what isn't your business," Helen snaps. "You think *I'm* happy that my mama's in the hospital?"

Shit, Theresa thinks. Not now. Oh God, I could deal with her before but not when she's like this. "Of course not, Mama," she says, turning to the window. Outside, it's almost noon. She's already late, had hoped to have been there an hour ago.

"Don't you humor me. I know what you're thinking."

Theresa continues facing the window, but she's alert for the first hint of movement. If she looks at Helen now it might be taken as a threat or, worse, a challenge. A worm of a memory from years ago sneaks to the front of her brain. An image of Helen enraged, eyes so wide that she could see the ring of soft red flesh around them, Helen coming after her for some misbehavior real or imagined, a kindling stick held so tightly in her hand that it took a week to pull the last splinter out. And she, Theresa, running in blind terror until Me-Maw heard the commotion and came running in to save her. Helen didn't get violent with Theresa often, but when she did, it was always Me-Maw who saved her.

A rustle from the couch, and Theresa instinctually pivots, splashing a few drops of coffee onto her sleeve, her arms raised to her chest. But Helen was just repositioning herself on the edge, her eyes narrow.

"Yeah, I've got you figured out," Helen says, nodding to herself. "You're just waiting so you can have me locked up in Broughton."

Without thinking Theresa slings what's left of her coffee into the sink, the mug along with it, and begins to protest. "Mama—"

"Don't you 'Mama' me, you little bitch. I've seen the way you look around my room, like you can't wait until I'm gone to start throwing everything away and make it nice for that little boyfriend of yours." Helen stands, jabbing in Theresa's direction with another cigarette, this one unlit, her previous one smoldering forgotten in the ashtray beside where she was sitting. "Selfish little cunt. You don't care about what happens in this house."

"Goddamnit, Mama," Theresa says, just barely loud enough for herself to hear. Me-Maw would be able to control Helen if she were here by pulling rank, reminding Helen that she was the elder, the wiser. But that won't work for Theresa. She just has to get out without upsetting Helen further.

"You think you're so fucking smart, don't you?" Helen continues, now with her new cigarette lit. A glowing pointer. "Well, let me tell you something. I still have control over what happens to me, and I'm not leaving."

"I know. No one is going to try and make you move, I promise," Theresa says, trying to keep herself calm. She can't react, not now. Later, when she's with Mark. She has to stay strong, like Me-Maw always said during one of Helen's fits. "But I have to go now."

"You're not going anywhere so you can talk about me. Tell those doctors lies about me." Helen charges suddenly, causing Theresa to flinch, but stops short at the metal strip that divides the cheap laminated flooring in the kitchen from the living room. "Besides," she laughs. "How you plan to get there? I've got the car keys." As if to prove her point she pulls the ring from the sweatpants' pocket and holds them out, shaking them like Theresa's a baby she's trying to distract.

Slowly, Theresa slides open the drawer in front of her, feeling around for the spare key to the Pontiac that Me-Maw had taped to the underside of the cabinet while keeping her eyes steady on Helen. She might have to push past her to make the door, but she hopes it won't come down to that. Her fingers find the grain of masking tape, sliding across until they touch metal.

"Mama, I have to go see Me-Maw now," she says, her voice flat, expressionless. As discreetly as she can she slides her clenched hand into her pocket. The coffee on top of empty stomach, save for what alcohol survived from the night before, comes back to collapse her gut against itself. But she can't deal with that now. She's almost free. "I'll tell her you love her, though."

"You're not listening!" Helen screams, but the cracks are beginning to show in her anger. She's wearing herself out. Theresa sees her chance and walks past her to the front door.

"It's okay, Mama. I'll be back later." Her hand is on the knob. She's almost there. She can feel the two metals: the one in her pocket now warm and slick with sweat, the knob still cool to the touch. "I put your medicine out for you. Take it and see if you don't feel better."

"They're leaving me," Helen says, turning her eyes to the overhead lamp, its shade speckled from inside with the carcasses of unnumbered flies. "They're going to leave me all alone to starve to death." A sob gets caught in her throat and she sits down right where she was standing, her knees hugged against herself.

Don't fall for it, Theresa thinks. It amazes her that after everything her first impulse is still to run over and wrap her arms around Helen, the prodigal daughter turned nurse who just wants to kiss her mother's boo-boos and make the pain go away. But that's never been her role. If Me-Maw were here she'd go and comfort Helen until she was calm enough to take her medicine, leaving Theresa to run to Mark to lick her wounds. But her Me-Maw is in the hospital, and she has to go.

"I'm sorry, Mama," she says, meaning more than just this morning, before opening the door and slipping out into the fall air, so clean it's like it was washed by the hills as it came to her. But Helen's cries follow her – hooks in the back – and she walks quickly to the car to begin the drive.

The volunteer at the information desk recognizes Theresa from before. Theresa sees her eyes narrow, the sideways glances magnified so much by her glasses that they have an unreal, cartoon-ish look.

"Can I help you?" the woman asks. They're the exact words she'd used when Theresa had first come in and gotten Me-Maw's room number, but now they sound guarded, hesitant.

Theresa wants to be offended, but she understands. There's no telling what she looks like to the woman, this proper hospital sentry with her floral blouse and graying hair spayed into a perm, a woman whose only job is to direct people to the right wing for a few hours between her garden club and Sunday morning service at one of the big downtown churches. Theresa has no way of knowing how much of Helen's wildness is in her eyes.

"I need to make a phone call," Theresa says.

"I'm sorry, this phone is for hospital use only." The woman's eyes continue to dart anywhere but on Theresa, but then they lock onto something in the lobby over Theresa's shoulder and she knows that one of the uniformed security guards must be standing there, acting nonchalant but watching nevertheless. "There's a courtesy phone in the cafeteria," the woman says, collecting herself enough to remember to smile. "It's on the third floor. I can have someone show you where it is, if you'd like."

Theresa thanks her and goes, hoping the guard she spies leaning against the wall doesn't come up and offer any token assistance. She doesn't have that much time. The nurse she'd spoken to – the one who'd found her staring at the empty hospital bed and told her Me-Maw was in surgery though not to worry – had said a doctor would stop by the room in a half-hour to explain, and she wants to be there waiting. But she can't wait alone, has done too much alone, she feels. She wants Mark.

It takes her a minute to find the cafeteria. All the hallways in Hopewell Memorial are the same – white walls, floors, and ceilings broken only by equally spaced doors and a narrow strip of mahogany wainscoting at waist level – and she's certain that several of the plastic signs have directional arrows that contradict other signs' arrows. But she finds it and, just to the inside of the door, the promised courtesy phone attached to the wall.

She dials quickly, then does it again remembering to dial nine. Mark answers on the second ring.

"It's me," she says, already feeling her need for him growing. If he doesn't come, if he's due at the school to watch the game tape or promised his parents he'd go with them on some errand, she's afraid she'll collapse on the spot, become another spill of bodily fluid for some poor orderly to mop up.

"What's wrong? Where *are* you?" It's mid-afternoon, and only a handful of doctors are eating at a table across the room. But the kitchen is in full swing, and the sounds of aluminum trays being stacked and shouts of employees carries across the space. She realizes that she hasn't eaten anything all day, but it's a realization without any real importance, like noticing your birthday is exactly two months away.

"The cafeteria at the hospital." She glances at the white, institutional clock, simultaneously cringing as the sound of metal slamming into metal erupts from behind the double doors across the room. She has about ten minutes, a little more, before the doctor is supposed to meet her at Me-Maw's room. "Can you meet me?" she asks.

There's a second's pause where she can hear Mark thinking. "Wait, at the cafeteria?" he asks. "Are you alright? Is Helen with you?"

She keeps herself calm enough to quickly explain, though barely. She wishes she could remember what the nurse told her the name of the surgery was. It sounded like angel-something, but it doesn't matter. It's happening to Me-Maw, right now inside this building, with Helen back at the house possibly still half-crazy. Theresa hopes she took the pills she'd laid out for her.

She calls home, the clock already telling her she should be on her way to meet the doctor, as soon as Mark hangs up. It rings four times before there's a click and Me-Maw's warbling voice, *"You've reached the Coffeys. We're not in..."*)

Theresa prays to Jesus or whoever is manning the lines that Helen is okay and rushes back into the webbed hallways towards the fifth floor and Me-Maw's room.

Mark gets there just ten minutes after the doctor. The doctor, a graying man with the polished-clean look and virgin-white robe of his profession, seems to sense something and pivots on his heels, allowing Theresa to see Mark framed in the doorway behind.

"Angioplasty," she says, immediately feeling stupid for blurting out the word the doctor had just finished explaining. A tube in Me-Maw's leg that somehow would help her heart, which the doctors believe had been having a series of minor heart attacks over the past few days due to her arteries narrowing, losing an elasticity Theresa hadn't known they possessed.

"Mark?" the doctor asks, glancing between him and Theresa. Then, almost under his breath he says, "Great game last night, son."

"Hey, Dr. Witherspoon." Mark shakes the man's hand before coming and sitting on the bed beside Theresa's chair. "How is she?" he asks Theresa.

"I was just telling Ms. Coffey here that her grandmother's been experiencing a series of minor heart attacks, but that we think the surgery will correct those. However, she will need to stay with us for a few days for observation. After that, we can transfer her to home care through Medicare, but she'll still need a lot of help around the house."

Without looking, Theresa can sense Mark nodding like she can sense him in the room. Just having him here, she can't explain the relief, as if his very presence is an arm wrapped around her.

The doctor turns, again facing Theresa from his standing position. "She may be more than you and your mother can handle, at least for a while. Have you considered a temporary facility?" he asks, a wince of hesitation to his voice. "Of course, that's something you would want to consider with your mother, but there are some really nice facilities in this area. A new one just opened up outside of town near John's River that's really top-notch."

Theresa nods and shakes the doctor's hand before he leaves, off to counsel another family, maybe one receiving worse news. As soon as he's gone, Mark's arm is around her and she buries herself in his chest. She tells him about Helen that morning, about how afraid she'd been until he got there, how she'd done it all herself. And as she does she feels the weight of it leaving her, his strength holding them both upright.

"It's going to be okay. I promise. As much as I can help it, we'll all be okay," Mark whispers into her hair.

The First Day It Felt Like Spring

Vernon guides Lucille down the long hallway leading from her room with his hand wrapped around the ball of her elbow. When it was built, the Vista House was looked down on some by those who thought "assisted living homes," as he found they liked to be called, should look like hospitals, with cheap linoleum floors, beige walls, and lots of contraptions beeping and squawking everywhere. At Vista, they'd designed most of the building to look like an old-fashioned mountain cabin with floors and walls of fake wormwood decorated with needlepoint and old oval portraits, and they'd put a wraparound porch out front with real wooden rocking chairs for the residents to visit in when the weather's nice.

Vernon thinks it was a great idea to decorate like this. All the doctors he'd talked to said that Alzheimer's patients did best in familiar surroundings, and he and Lucy both had been born and raised on neighboring farms nearby on the western side of Hopewell County, both farms tucked into the bottomland where John's River spills down from the Blue Ridge between Brown Mountain and Collettsville. Only the hallway at Vista resembles the antiseptic dreariness of a doctor's office, and Vernon hurries his wife outside if only to escape it himself.

She'll be alright once he gets her out onto the porch, but he's afraid of what would happen if she were to take too much stock of her surroundings right now. It's a long walk, and he has to move slowly, deliberately to keep Lucy from trying to wander. By the time they reach the front door, he already knows he'll need to ice his knee down tonight if he hopes to walk tomorrow.

It's the first time since last fall they've been able to hold their visit outside. Spring was early this year, and now it's barely April and the air's already taken on the radiance of summer, where the sun heats the air until it expands like a bag of microwave popcorn. Like the air always felt in the factory.

"Tell me again why you're not in town?" Lucy asks.

"Honey, I've told you time and again that I'm retired now."

She seems to relax, the small amount of muscle remaining in her arm loosening against his grip as he guides her to a rocker. "Oh, good," she says, smiling. "I was afraid they'd fired you. You know how bad we need that money."

They'd built Vista at the top of a small rise, giving the porch and dining hall a fine view of the valley where Tucker lies mostly hidden under a canopy of new leaves. Beyond the far side of town, Killdary looms like a forlorn watchtower, much in the same way it had when he and Lucy were young and they would sit on her Daddy's porch on summer evenings visiting and, in years when the crops were looking good, listen to her father fiddle at the darkening sky.

"Remember when your Daddy used to play on that fiddle for us?" he asks, but when he turns to face his wife, she's staring off into the middle distance, a thin smile growing across her face.

"Lord, it's hot," she says. "Help me out of this here sweater, will you?"

He knows it'll only hasten her back inside, but he complies, leaning over to help Lucille tug her arms out of the woolen sleeves. Thank God she still has her strength, he thinks, before wondering which she'd prefer if given the choice: her strength or her mind.

"Don't you remember, Lucy? Your Mama would fix a little icemilk and we'd sit there and listen to him play and her sing?"

"You hate icemilk. Say it makes you sick."

Vernon ignores the remark and leans forward, resting his forearms across his thighs to look into his wife's face, so similar to his own now that age has left their skin hanging loose to show the lines of their skulls beneath. She was so beautiful back then. Her eyes follow him, but he can't tell anymore what she hears and what she doesn't. He continues to try, some days more than others, and today she'd remembered his name, recognized him from somewhere beneath the age.

"Remember?" he asks. At the time, he'd hated those evenings. Hated driving all that way from town just to sit around jawing with Lucy's father and brothers while she helped in the kitchen. All he'd wanted was a few minutes to talk to her alone, a few minutes' peace and maybe a kiss. But it had worked out all right in the end, and now when he turns on the radio there doesn't seem to be anything as good as the songs they'd sung back on that porch.

"God, he knew them all. 'Barbara Allen,' 'Wind Done Gone,' 'Shady Grove' and more reels than I can remember."

He watches Lucy's face for some sense that she's hearing the same old songs in her own head, but her eyes have wandered over his shoulder.

"It's lovely today," she says. "I'm so glad you're working up in the drafting office now. I hear it gets so hot on that floor that grown men are liable to pass out."

"I already told you once today, I retired."

An edge of irritation slips into Vernon's voice. For a minute, he'd imagined they were having a real conversation.

Lucille stares up at Killdary in the distance, crossing her arms over her chest and refusing to look in his direction.

"I'm cold," she says. "Take me inside."

Vernon stares down, studying the boards beneath his feet. Notch and groove, probably walnut. Expensive, but good, sturdy wood for flooring.

Where You Are From

It happened when Vernon was just getting to the point he felt confident. When he'd first been hired, the shop foreman had watched over Vernon like a stern guardian angel, helping him learn to measure the space between drillings by sight, watching him load the clampings to make certain there wouldn't be any give when the bit strove into the wood. A stick of lumber not properly clamped could lead to a broken drill bit or, worse, a slung piece of wood. Either meant almost certain injury if not death for any man caught in the way. With the Depression's effects creeping further and further south, the company could afford to replace a worker pretty easily, but things weren't as easy for those injured.

Vernon had left home with his father's blessing. Even with the TVA stringing electricity up into the hollows the farm hadn't been producing what it once did, and besides, it had been decided a long time before that the farm would go to Vernon's oldest brother when the time came. Not that he was complaining. His father had raised him up hard, but Vernon couldn't say he'd been unfair. He'd let Vernon go to the valley school when he wasn't busy with farm work. He'd taught him that a man couldn't afford to worry about much other than himself and his family and that God made no promises that life wouldn't test how much a man could handle. So, in the fall of his sixteenth year he'd taken a room at a house in town and found work apprenticing on the drill press, guiding a three-eighths-inch bit in its rise and fall for six to ten hours a day, depending on the orders.

And Vernon felt pretty good about the situation after the first eighteen months or so. He could guide a sanded table leg into the clamps and drill the dowel holes in less than ten seconds, all with hardly a glance at his fingers.

More importantly, getting on at the plant proved to Lucy's daddy that Vernon could be trusted to care for a wife and family. He'd been courting Lucille Coffey ever since he got old enough to notice the little girl who liked to spend her idle time in the far corners of the Coffey farm, where a common fence was all that separated the two plots. He spent his days at the factory daydreaming about the way her hair looked like flax in the sun and how it fell in waves across her round shoulders when she felt free enough to let it down, and about how damn pretty her eyes were, like ponds at first light.

And while living in town, Vernon still drove the forty-five minutes across the old wagon roads to the valley just to see her for a few hours on Sunday afternoons and the occasional summer evening when he could borrow the old Model A from his landlord. He'd almost saved up enough for an apartment to put their marriage bed in when the accident happened.

As much as he's thought about it, Vernon still doesn't remember throwing that wood. He remembers the day, remembers how it was just at the tail end of the summer of nineteen forty-one. It was upwards of ninety degrees in the open air, which would've put it at well over a hundred and ten under the rafters in the machine room. Even with all the windows open for ventilation and the fans running full, the entire room seemed choked with sweat and sawdust. He recalls how just in front of his drill, the dark sweat stain on the back of Fat Joe Miller started spreading like a bloodstain and the air seemed to swirl. Vernon remembers a particular sliver of dust, a splinter he saw in such detail that he was able to pick out each fiber in its natural weave against the gun-metal of the drill.

And then he was on the floor with bodies and faces pressing against him, and his leg was a knot of fire.

There's a pack of men at the counter when Vernon walks into the Omelet King, the Waffle House clone on US-321 that acts as the daytime gathering place for the retired and unemployed. Some of the men he knows vaguely, and some he doesn't know at all. He spots Lucas

Where You Are From

Shook nodding along to a conversation at one end next to an empty stool and makes his way down, easing himself up to the counter.

The waitress, a plump young woman with her hair permed into a ball atop her head and a thin pink scar running the length of her chin, comes to take Vernon's order while he and Lucas say their hellos, catch up on their respective families. Up until a year before, Lucas was the shop foreman at Hill-Dale # 7. The two men had met in a waiting room at Hopewell Memorial while their wives had tests and had bonded over their common employer and the fact that each had only fathered a single child, which, Vernon thinks, was rarer then than now. The preliminaries end in mutual silent nods, and he watches as Lucas taps a cigarette butt-first on the countertop before bringing it to his lips and lighting it.

Vernon slides down off the stool and walks the length of the restaurant to the bathrooms. His knee is tender when he sits down on the cool lid of the toilet. Sometimes he worries that he's mourning Lucy before he's lost her, and he just has to take a minute to himself.

By the time he comes out again the men's conversation has increased in volume, and Vernon catches the name Clinton as he passes by. He figures the men are arguing over that business with the intern, and he remembers a time when such matters weren't aired for public consumption.

"What do you make of it?" Lucas leans over and asks under his breath, nodding the back of his head at the crowd.

"Clinton? Don't like the man, but I figure that what he did with that young lady is between him and his wife."

Lucas sucks hard on the cigarette then stubs it out. "Hell, not that. The talk about NAFTA finally shutting down all the plants and moving them to Mexico."

Vernon has heard the rumors for the past several years, ever since NAFTA was signed into law, but in his experience rumors circulate more in good times than in bad. Still, he isn't in the mood to get drawn in. Sometimes the old men just come down to pick a fight, let off some steam just like they used to do at the bars and roadhouses in Rhyne when they were younger.

"Heck," he says, watching the skinny cook toss a handful of hash browns onto the grill beside his cheeseburger. "It looks like they're coming here. Just the other day I saw another sign offering jobs in Spanish."

Lucas laughs, knocking his fist on the table for emphasis. "I knew you'd say I was right. I been trying to tell these fellows that Mr. Hill ain't going to close down shop in the same town that made him what he is, but they get these ideas in their heads, and–"

"Now wait a second, Luke," Vernon interrupts. Lucas has attracted attention from the other end of the counter, and they watch with narrowed, smirking eyes.

He drops his voice. "I was just stating my opinion. It don't mean I'm right."

"Yeah, but you'd know better than anyone else here," Lucas says. "You're the one who worked up there with the managers. I was just a shop foreman."

"That don't mean I know nothing more than you do," Vernon says. He can sense the men's ears reaching from behind Lucas, and as the waitress lays the plate of food before him, he wishes he'd asked her for it to go. "I grew up a dirt farmer just like you, and just because they sat me at a fancy table and gave me a pencil to work with don't mean they were telling me their secrets."

"Yeah, but that son-in-law of yours works over there, don't he?"

If the men weren't paying attention before, Vernon knows they are now. He wants to direct their attention away from him, but especially away from asking after his son-in-law, who's currently traveling with investors in China. The men would have a field day if he let *that* fact slip, although Hill-Dale has been sending men to sweet-talk money out of

Where You Are From

Europeans for years.

Besides, Vernon's never felt comfortable around his son-in-law, who he finds aloof and distant, a man who stands on his deck and makes small talk about the work he plans to have done on the house. Even when Jason was just another boy Linda was bringing home from Boone, Vernon had found him a bit off-putting. He'd been shocked to find that his little girl had a boyfriend who slicked his hair back with gel and wore sports jackets to family dinners before he could legally drink, even more shocked when Jason announced his intention one evening to become a successful businessman in order to get into politics. To Vernon, modesty was and is still a virtue, pride still the deadliest of all sins.

"Yeah, what do you hear about it?" one of the men demands, poking his whiskered face in their direction.

"I don't hear anything. Just stating my opinion, fellows. Remember how worked up everyone got after the war? Everyone figuring that there weren't enough jobs for everybody?" He's trying to backpedal, but as soon as Vernon hears himself mention the war he cringes. He hadn't meant to bring it up, avoids the subject whenever possible, doesn't even watch the History Chanel because of it. But now he's opened the door.

The man who spoke before leans even further forward. "Yeah, I remember," he says, glancing down at the floor with his face so screwed up that for a minute Vernon's worried he'll spit on it. "Came back from the Navy in forty-six and found out my saw had been taken by some poor bastard that hadn't even had the guts to sign up in the first place. Had to start back in the varnish room for damn near six months waiting for a spot to open back up in assembly."

Several of the men nod, and the man looks them all over in turn before turning back to Vernon. In the man's eyes is a challenge Vernon can't meet.

"Hey now, what the hell's wrong with the varnish room?" Lucas says, and Vernon finds himself temporarily spared.

Lucas squares his shoulders and pulls his metal lighter from his pocket, making a show of lighting his next cigarette. "When I came back from France I was more than happy to get back on in there." He sets the lighter down, one end then the other so it snaps against the counter. On the face is a red oval crossed with a pattern of blue with the words *Old Hickory* stamped underneath.

The whiskered man recedes by a margin invisible but plain to anyone in the room. "There ain't nothing *wrong* with it; it just wasn't my saw."

"I know a man spent his whole working life in the varnish room. Has to carry an oxygen tank," another man adds, but his voice is soft, disarming. "Good man, too."

No one pays him any mind.

The first man looks up with a new spark, but the fight's already gone out of his voice. "And, hell, it wasn't where they put me; just that they didn't put me back where I'd been after I'd been off fighting for this country. A man shouldn't profit off another man's service like that; wait 'til he's gone and move in for his job. Now *that's* what was wrong with it."

The entire group mulls that over. After a minute, Lucas nods and concedes, "Well, I see your point there," ending the discussion.

Vernon looks at the plate in front of him. The food is still warm, the heat from the circle of meat moistening the bun and making it soft, gummy. He puts five dollars on the counter, checks his math in his head, and pulls out another dollar, laying it beside the first. Linda should still be at the school where she works as a librarian, and he decides he can catch her if he leaves now.

"You ain't going to eat that?" Lucas asks, pointing with the tip of his cigarette.

"Eyes were bigger than my stomach. Take it if you want." Vernon slides himself off the counter and waves to the waitress. "Money's on the counter," he calls.

Where You Are From

The sun's reflection off the cars is nearly blinding after the orange filter of the restaurant's pulled blinds. The air radiates the sun's energy, but Vernon's face feels cool in the breeze, and, although he hasn't eaten, his stomach feels knotted like he'd just finished a steak that wasn't sitting right. He looks at his car, a new but nondescript gray Lincoln, and wonders if he shouldn't have driven the old Buick a little while longer. The longer Vernon stands, the more conscious he is of his knee, and so he slowly makes his way to the car and joins the traffic that clogs the highway every day at the end of Hill-Dale's first shift, the splintered men and women who make up nearly half the county's workforce smoking cigarettes with their windows down, probably feeling the first fresh air they'd breathed since early in the morning.

Vernon had tried to enlist when the war came; he wasn't a coward. He knew he wasn't fit for front line service, but he figured the army had to have some use for him. The doctors had told him how close he'd come to losing the leg altogether – it had only been a matter of luck that gifted him a shattered knee instead of a shredded one – and within three months of the accident he was already up on his feet, albeit with a crutch.

So, he'd left the farm for the first time since the accident with his middle brother Robert only to wait nearly two hours in line for the recruiter to take one glance at him, one peek into his medical chart, and immediately declare him 4-F, leaving him with a sullen ride back spent listening to Robert boast about the hordes of Japs and Krauts he planned to kill.

But by D-Day Vernon's life was beginning to take shape again. After slinking back to the farm a certified cripple he'd almost given up hope. He'd tried to help with the planting that spring, but his knee wasn't healed enough for the constant bending, and he'd wound up bedridden for two weeks as reward for his effort. So, when Mr. Coffey came bearing word that Hill-Dale was looking for men with a little schooling to train as drafters, all theirs being drawn into the military as engineers, he'd jumped at the chance.

Vernon had done well in math at the valley school and knew how to figure most calculations out with pencil and paper, but that didn't keep the nerves down when he went into the main office to apply. And for a while after he'd gotten the job, beating out two Lord's Creek women and an old black janitor from Tucker's North End, he'd still felt like an imposter sitting at the big, angled table with the oversized sheets of drafting paper spread out before him. They had to show him how to use a T-square and how to account for variables in lumber supply due to the war effort, but it hadn't taken long for him to catch on.

With a steady job, one that paid better than running a drill ever would, he'd been able to marry Lucille and put a down payment on a small bungalow between downtown and the office. And when the war ended, he'd been kept on as a drafter, working steady and providing for Lucille and, after nineteen forty-seven, Linda as best he could.

He'd tried to remember what his father had taught him about a man's loyalties, seeing Linda through four years at the teaching college in Boone and laying the financial framework for his eventual old age, and did his best to forget the luck and chance that had made it possible. You can only play the cards that are dealt, he thought whenever his mind wandered to the man whose job he'd taken at the table, a man who'd lost his life building a bridge in some Pacific jungle. He'd done the best he could. He'd never asked for the accident, had never thought that the puzzles and number games he played in the two-room school would see him into a career where he wore a tie to work and could buy into the stock market. It wasn't his fault, no matter what folks had called him during those years. They couldn't hold him responsible.

Driving down the Westside Highway, Vernon recognizes the names of all the cross streets, but he can't seem to place the names of the few businesses left along this stretch. It's unsettling, like looking through familiar family photos with strangers' names written on the backs. Just the other week he'd stopped by the old StarGrille Diner hoping that the new owner had kept at least the fried okra from the old menu. The building had looked the same from the parking lot, long and narrow like an old railroad depot and painted the same dark shade of blue that camouflaged the coat of dirt spat by the nearby smokestacks, but inside he'd been disappointed to find that both the okra and oilcloth covered tables were gone, replaced by fake-wood Formica and hamburgers wrapped in the same paper they use at the fast-food chains along 321. It wasn't until later that he remembered he'd used to joke that the okra was fried to hide the fact it was rotten. Made him wonder what the hell he'd been thinking of stopping in the first place.

    Vernon stops at a red light and looks through a chain-link fence at the blank red brick wall of Hill-Dale #4, watching men and women move along the outside. When he was young it was only men, white men at that, who were given jobs working the machines, but that changed with the war. During those four long years the company had opened its doors to anyone willing to work – black or white, man or woman – and afterwards things just stayed that way. There had been some worry at the time that there weren't going to be enough jobs to go around, but aside from gripes like the man at the Omelet King it hadn't come to much. And just like he told the man, now it seems they can't get enough workers, even with all the Mexicans moving into town. Right beside the clapboard guard shack the sign still proclaims: NOW HIRING / OFERTA DE TRABAJO.

    When he gets to thinking about it, the factories are the only things in West Tucker that haven't changed completely. His house in Upper Creek, the split-level with the gazebo in the backyard, hadn't existed when he and Lucille were raising Linda. It had just been a part of the old Miller farm, with another farm separating the plot from the

Wilkesboro Highway where the land begins to rise up the north face of Killdary Mountain. Now those farms are gone, replaced by what Vernon guesses are suburbs, although the area is officially inside the city limits: neighborhoods with bike lanes and grocery stores, the maple and oak saplings planted back when the land was first broken into subdivisions now tall and thick-trunked. The people who still live in West Tucker are either old timers clinging to homes bought fifty years ago, young workers just starting out at the plants, or those who can't afford to live anywhere else. Hell, now half of the buildings downtown are boarded up or else have been bulldozed and turned into parking lots that remain empty, the town's commerce now centered around the overcrowded shopping centers on 321 leading north towards Boone. Vernon remembers sitting on a stretch of sidewalk and listening to Doc Watson play before anyone knew who Doc Watson was, a sidewalk that's now cracked and littered with empty bottles, some still in paper sacks, and seeded with cigarette butts. He wonders if Lucy ever has memories of town, if sometimes she finds her mind wandering down Main Street when it was crowded with Saturday shoppers. If she did, he decides in the end, she'd probably just remember the soot from the old coal furnaces gathered in the corners of windows, the dark and ugly.

"Hey, Daddy!" Linda looks up, her eyes magnified by prescription glasses, when she sees Vernon standing awkwardly in the library doorway.

"Hope I'm not bothering you," he says. "I was just driving around and thought I'd stop by."

The library is vacant save for Vernon and his daughter, the students having been released a half-hour before. It amazes him every time he visits Linda here how small the room is – no bigger than a regular classroom – yet it never feels crowded. There are empty gaps on every shelf, even though the shelves don't stretch all the way around the room.

Where You Are From

The empty spaces are filled by posters of celebrities with encouraging messages about reading. He wonders if this same room was used for a library back when the building was the black high school and, if it was, if the selections were as sparse then, too.

"You don't have to stand in the doorway, Daddy. I was just finishing up here." Linda writes one last thing down in a ledger and pushes a button on the computer monitor before stepping around the desk to hug him.

As a child, Linda had favored him, with the same dark hair and stern, knife-blade features. Now in her fifties, she reminds him of Lucille more and more. Her hair turned gray early just like Lucille, and her face had rounded out after the birth of her daughter, now a junior at UNC. She smells different, though, and her clothes are nicer. Lucille always smelled like the hills to him: a light grassy scent with a touch of iron, but his daughter smells as inoffensively indistinct as new carpet. Her clothes have the pressed and polished sheen of wealth that, despite his office job, Vernon could never afford to give his own wife.

Linda stares into his eyes as their hug loosens in stages. For a second it's as if he's staring into Lucille's years before, back when there was something more behind them than broken fragments. So, she has her mother's eyes now, too, he thinks.

"Daddy, are you okay?"

They face each other across one of the library's long tables. The late afternoon light spills in through the tall windows, painting the room with a graying, deadened light. Outside, the parking lot is empty except for the Lincoln and the new Audi Linda had gotten for her last anniversary. Northside Middle, having been Old North High, is located in the dead center of Tucker's largest black neighborhood, and until the city built the new MLK Recreation Center it had been the community's gathering place, its de facto city hall. But this afternoon the campus is silent except for the sounds leaking across the border from the neighborhood beyond: the rumblings of a car stereo, the shrieks and laughter of children's games.

"How is Maria doing down east?" he asks.

"She's fine, Daddy. Thinking of changing her major again, but fine." Linda glances at a clock hanging somewhere above his head. She folds her hands together on the table before them, like she had as a teenager when she came to borrow money or the car.

"What is she studying, again?"

"Biology, but now she's thinking of becoming an anthropology major, if you can imagine." She smiles, but her lips quickly fold into themselves. "That's not what you want to talk about, though. Is it about Mom?"

"No, no. Your mother is, well, she actually seemed a little better today when I went out there."

Linda lets out a breath Vernon hadn't realized she was holding. "You scared me there for a minute," she says.

"I wanted to ask what Jason was doing in China."

"I told you before he left, remember? He went with a potential investor."

"I thought he was meeting the investor there. Why would he take an investor to China?"

Linda sighs and gives him the same gabled-eyebrow look of patient understanding he remembers from living with her. It's one of the few traits Vernon can't trace back to either himself or Lucille, one that probably proves useful to her at the middle school.

"He didn't take the investor over there. Jason met him in Chicago and then they flew over there together."

"But why?" Vernon worries that he sounds pleading and makes a note to be more careful.

"I'm not sure of all the details, really," she leans across the table towards him, her eyes alight with gossip. "But it looks like Mr. Hill is going to join the company into a conglomerate."

Vernon nods, swallows. He hadn't really believed it, had thought it was just the power of old men's worry.

"What's that mean?" he asks.

"From what I understand, not much. Mr. Hill is getting on in years and the company's grown so big it's hard for him to keep running it by himself."

"What's going to happen around here?" he asks.

"Nothing, as far as I know." Linda leans back, looks at him sidelong. "Daddy, are you sure you're okay?"

"Then why is Jason in China?" he asks. Why not just meet the man in Chicago?"

"Because the conglomerate is looking at building a few factories there." For the first time since they sat down, Linda's eyes leave him. "Look, Daddy, they aren't going to close down any plants."

Vernon wants to ask why she won't look him in the eye, why she mentioned the possibility of the plants closing at all if it wasn't going to happen. He's surprised he doesn't feel anger, though, simply flustered, like he does when he can't make out what someone is saying to him over the phone.

Linda speaks first. "Jason says that if Mr. Hill sells, he wants a clause in the contract that still calls for most of the control to be local. It'll still be Hill-Dale, and the offices here in town will stay open." She starts to play with a bracelet Vernon hadn't seen in years, a gold charm bracelet she'd been given for her Sweet Sixteen.

Vernon points to the bracelet. "I didn't know you still had that."

Linda looks up, placing her wrist in the middle of the table like a centerpiece. She smiles meekly at him, and he returns the gesture. "Of course, I do," she says.

Christopher Lee Nelson

On the way home, Killdary fills the top half of his windshield, the sun making the bare branches on the west face shine like amber. It will be Easter soon, and then the mountain will turn green again. At Vista, Lucille should be in her room waiting on dinner, and Vernon wonders if she's looking out the window, if she's seeing the same thing.

Karissa's Weekend

I'm late. I'd agreed to meet Jason in the parking lot of the West Tucker Food-Lion at six thirty, but it was already six twenty-five when Jennifer dropped me off at home. According to my dashboard clock, it's seven fifteen when I park beside Jason's silver Lexus.

"Where the fuck were you? I tried to call three times." He's at my side as soon as I open the door. Although it's only in the mid-60's, there's a thin line of sweat on his upper lip and his ordinarily tight curls look mussed and uncombed.

"I had to talk to my Mom."

In fact, Mom hadn't even batted an eye when I ran through the kitchen on the way to get my bags, and when I told her that I was spending the night at Jennifer's all she said was, "Have fun, dear." She was cooking, which usually means she has a date with some teacher or artist-type that happened to wander past her desk at the Art Council and is happy to have the house to herself. Since the divorce last year, we've been fairly content to allow each other our own lives.

"Well, I was getting worried," Jason huffs as he tosses my duffle bag into the trunk.

"Sorry." I go ahead and let myself in, slumping in the seat and lighting a cigarette even though he's asked me not to smoke in the car.

"Where are we staying?" We've just gotten on the interstate outside Morganton, about a half-hour away from Tucker.

"The Best Western downtown." Jason's eyes cut to me, then away. Neither of us have said much, only clipped sentences about bathroom stops and the like. He must catch my rolled eyes because the corner of his lip tightens. "Look, do you have any idea how hard it was to get away for the night?"

"How *is* Linda, by the way?"

His eyes widen like he's been slapped.

"She's fine."

I nod and stare out the window. The scenery's just one big blur of green.

After a minute I turn back to him. "I'm sorry."

"It's alright," he's nearly whispering, his voice a thin line of gravel at the bottom of his throat. "I know this has to be hard on you." He turns and faces me, giving me a good view of his brown eyes, and for a second I'm reminded of six months ago – when we were new and he was full of compassion, when I could talk to him for hours without him once making me feel like a little kid, back when I used to think there might be something more between us than a married real estate executive fucking an eighteen-year-old.

"Are you sure you want me to do this?" The question unexpectedly falls out of my mouth like a piece of gum chewed too long.

"Absolutely." He stops, realizing he's spoken too quickly. "I mean, I wish this didn't have to happen …"

"But there isn't another choice." I finish the sentence for him.

We're climbing the ridge that separates Asheville from the foothills below. Outside Jason's window, waves of blue-green ridges stretch until they vanish in the southern haze, but on my side there's only the sheer rock face where the highway was carved from the shoulder of the mountain.

I'm not prepared for Asheville. I'd expected it to be a lot like Tucker, only bigger, where the only people downtown are old or leaned against doorways hugging brown paper bags, but here the sidewalks are full of kids my age and the beggars actually beg. A mohawked couple sits on a curb with bent cigarettes hanging from their lips. A cluster of girls in wrap skirts sprawl across a bench. A man in a tattered camouflage jacket and bright orange wig staggers up to them and leaves a minute later, clutching something to his chest and muttering. And everywhere, *everywhere*, young men and women push strollers.

"What time's the appointment?" I ask on the patio of a restaurant on the square that calls its food Oriental-fusion.

"Ten o'clock. Before lunch." Jason takes another swig of rice wine and grimaces. "Jesus, this shit is strong," he mumbles. It's his fourth glass. I realize that he's drunk. I take a drag off my cigarette, not quite as hungry as before.

"Does the clinic know?"

"As far as they're concerned, you're my niece." He looks around quickly. The patio tables are all smashed together, ten occupying a space big enough for four, but we're the only ones left outside at nine-thirty.

"Goddamn."

"What?"

"Just that you're so paranoid." I wish he'd show half the concern for me that he shows for his reputation, but I guess I shouldn't complain. Empathy. Try to see this from his side, how frightened he must be. Stay in control. Otherwise, all hell could break loose.

He nods, then stares down to where his fingertips meet the tablecloth. "What did you mean earlier, in the car?" he asks.

Somehow I know exactly what he's talking about. "I don't know."

"You meant *something*."

The waiter interrupts him, and I snub my cigarette out underneath my heel. But as soon as the waiter leaves Jason presses the issue.

"I thought you agreed this was best," he says, leaning across the table with more intensity than necessary. He smells like stale bread.

"It is best." I give up the pretense of hunger and set my crossed chopsticks along the rim of the bowl. "But that doesn't mean I have to like it."

"I don't want you to hate me," he says, staring straight at me. "Please don't hate me." *Or tell my wife,* I think. *Or come to my church and stand up confessing during the offertory. Or follow any other cliché of the scorned mistress and fuck up my life.*

"Stop worrying," I say, staring at the waiter.

But Jason won't let it drop.

"You're going to tell people, aren't you?" This back at the hotel after dinner. I'm trying to talk him into sleeping while he sits on the edge of the bed drenched in sweat.

"I will if you don't shut up." This isn't a joke. The only way I'll have the strength to go through with the operation is if I don't think about it. Like a booster shot at the pediatrician's office – close your eyes and it will all be over before you know it, a pat on the head and a lollypop for being such a big girl. But there seems to be less air in the room than there should be, and I wonder if this is how lightning bugs feel when they're in a kid's Mason jar.

Eventually Jason goes into the bathroom, and after a minute I can hear him moaning above the hum of the fan. I take the opportunity, careful to slip one of the plastic key-cards into my pocket before letting the door close as softly as possible behind me.

It's late, but I want to get as far away from that room as possible, so I duck down the first alley I come to and aim myself towards what I think is the center of town. The alley's deserted, although distorted guitars and badly out-of-time drums echo off the walls from an unseen window. The air is cool with a touch of moisture. I realize that for the first time all weekend, I have no plan. I could just start walking and disappear.

The alley empties into a crowded, wide boulevard. Couples pass arm-in-arm without pause. Larger groups part and momentarily surround me before rejoining on the other side.

I see the sign of a coffee-shop two blocks down. It looks inviting: a warm yellow light spilling out, clusters of people milling around the entrance. I order a black coffee and find a booth with a view of the street. Although most of the crowd is my age, kids too young for the bars but too old to stay home, I feel noticeably out of place. The mood is too light, too happy. A girl in a pink tank-top and heels laughs loudly at something her dreadlocked boyfriend says and I want to slap her. The longer I nurse the coffee the tighter the screw in my chest turns. I feel quarantined, cancerous, and I hate it.

"You look pissed." A boy appears across from me, sliding into the booth with a smile. I'm not in the mood for conversation.

"What if I am?"

"Come on," he knocks the table twice, "on a beautiful night like tonight?"

I roll my eyes, though it doesn't seem to faze him. He takes a sip from the drink he brought and gives me the smile again. "Boy problems?" he asks.

I don't answer, but I find myself not wanting him to leave. Not quite yet, at least.

"Girl problems?" He leans across the table, lifting a coy eyebrow and stretching his voice into a carnival barker's enticement. He's definitely cute. His hair's blond and spiked with something that shines in the overhead light, and his eyes are a gorgeous shade of bluish-green. But it's his smile I like the most. It's pure, and despite his showmanship it doesn't seem to be a façade.

"No," I giggle. I can't help it.

"Then what?"

"Nothing. It's nothing." I shake my head to clear it. "I'm Karissa."

"Dell." He reaches across the table and shakes my hand. His grip is firm, but his skin is soft and uncalloused.

§

"So you really haven't been here before?"

"Nope."

I stare up at the monument, a granite phallus with *VANCE* carved across the base. Despite the city lights, a few stars glow dimly above the pinnacle. Over my shoulder is the same restaurant where Jason and I'd eaten, but it seems like something from a distant and nearly forgotten dream.

"Well, this is historic Pack Square," Dell says, standing and sweeping his arm out like a game-show host. "And this," he points to the monument, "was erected to commemorate North Carolina's first and only Confederate Governor, Zebulon Vance, a Buncombe County native."

I applaud when he's finished. "Not bad."

"I worked as a tour guide last summer," he grins, sitting back down next to me, a few inches closer than he was before.

"You're lucky to live here."

"I know." He pauses and looks into my eyes. In the streetlamps' yellow glow his eyes are dark marble. I become conscious of my heartbeat. "So, you just here for the weekend, or longer?"

"Just the weekend."

"By yourself? With parents?"

The image of Jason forces itself into my mind for the first time since Dell appeared. "I'm visiting my uncle."

"Cool. Where's he live?" Dell leans back, spreading his arms along the back of the concrete bench. He glances between me and the buildings around us.

Jason's face fights its way to the front of my mind, causing me to swallow. His slate eyes, his slowly wrinkling brow crumpled into his hands at the edge of a stained hotel bed; I see it stretching into shock and fear when I gave him the news, looming over me with the delighted, grit-teeth stare of orgasm. But he's not here.

We wind up in Dell's apartment. It's not big, just a few rooms carved from a labyrinthine maze of hallways in a Victorian a few blocks north of the interstate, nor is it immaculate or even that clean. But it has a lived-in feel that I like. The walls are painted dark green, and books are stacked by the doorway to the bedroom. Posters for Led Zeppelin and some band called Built to Spill hang above a small stereo. There aren't any windows in the living room, but I can forgive that.

"I love your place."

"Thanks," he leans over the edge of the couch, and I hear a drawer sliding open. "How old did you say you were, again?" he asks.

"Eighteen."

"You smoke?"

"You know I do."

His face clouds before it breaks into his joker's grin. "I mean pot. Do you get high?" He pulls out a pipe about six inches long and sets it on the table. The stuff in the bowl is pale green with flecks of orange. I've seen weed before, but it was either rolled into a joint or else brown and coarse. This stuff looks more like moss. I think of the reason for coming to Asheville in the first place, but it feels like something separate, apart from the moment.

Dell hands me the pipe along with a lighter. I set the flame to the bowl and inhale, but the flame doesn't take.

"Hold the carb," he giggles, leaning across my lap and pointing out a small hole I'd missed on the side of the pipe. As much as I'm embarrassed, I enjoy the feeling of his body against mine.

I cover it and try again. This time, the flame takes and the weed grows bright ginger. I must hit it too hard, though, because as soon as I finish, something catches in my throat, and I start coughing and can't stop.

"Good shit, eh? I got it off this guy I know, fresh from B.C."

I nod like I know what he's talking about. He, in turn, gets up and seems to glide to the stereo. Jangling guitars and a nasally male voice fill the room. I'm not sure if it's the weed, but I start to feel like I stuck my head inside a plastic bag for too long.

Dell sits and takes the pipe, his knee keeping time. "What do you think?" he asks, exhaling a perfect column of smoke and nodding towards the music.

"What is it?"

"Built to Spill."

"It's pretty good." It wouldn't be my first choice for the moment – I think I'd prefer something more romantic, like Ella Fitzgerald or Patsy Cline – but the longer I listen the more the music makes sense. The rattling melodies swim in and out of my head. Dell passes the pipe back and it sounds even better.

"Actually, I think I'm really starting to get into it."

Dell flashes his wonderful smile again and leans in. His tongue wraps around mine like a serpent, setting off a lightning storm inside my chest. I want him. More than I've wanted anyone ever before.

I pull away, a hesitation before losing myself. "Goddamn," I hiss.

He moans and reaches for me. I push him against the arm of the sofa and straddle him as he sets the pipe on the table and weaves his arms through mine, his hands coming to rest on my shoulders.

"Hold on a second." He stands and goes into the bedroom. When he reappears, the neon-colored plastic of a condom wrapper peeking out from his fist, my shirt and bra are already on the floor.

"Are you sure you want this?" he asks.

"Absolutely."

I take his arm and guide the condom down onto the table. Later, I'll have to make my way back to the hotel and Jason, endure whatever, but this moment here, with Dell hovering over me like a vision, is mine alone.

What He Knows

"Dad! Dad!"

Carl Shook listens to his son's voice echo across the empty parking lot, off the tall brick wall and back again, hollow. The large rusty sign is still attached to the top of the wall, at least fifty feet off the ground, in large block letters: HILL-DALE ASSEMBLY #7.

Carl doesn't respond. It takes all his energy to keep his hold on the chain link fence separating the lot from the old plant. His fingers show the ragged cross-stitches earned inside that building from years handling rough wood, sanding each piece down until it was smooth enough for final assembly. The life he'd been prepared for. Behind him, the traffic flowing by on Westside Highway sounds like wind you hear coming but hasn't reached you yet.

"Didn't you hear me?" Doug appears at his father's side. He's unnaturally tall for his age. He hit his first growth spurt early, in fourth grade, and two years later he's just a foot or so shorter than Carl's six feet. Carl wishes Doug would try basketball again. He'd be sure to make the middle school's team next year if he practiced, but the boy says he doesn't want to.

"I heard you."

"Mom wants to know what you're doing out here."

"What are you doing here?" Carl asks. "Why aren't you in school?"

"I had a doctor's appointment, and we were driving home and saw your truck." The boy keeps talking, spilling inane details about the appointment and school, and something about stopping at McDonald's.

Carl nods, keeping his eyes focused on the wall. He'd forgotten about Doug's check-up. "Everything go okay?" he asks, interrupting.

"I guess."

Carl nods again. Another hundred or so dollars spent, and the boy's healthy. He'd told Karen to take him to the Health Department. She, of course, had wanted Carl to take Doug to the doctor, but he'd refused. That kind of stuff was for a mother. Work was for a father. That's how it had been at his house growing up. It's the way things have always been.

Carl doesn't move, and, after a minute, Doug turns and walks back to the waiting car. Carl listens as the engine cranks and the sound of crunching gravel fades into the white noise of the highway.

The house is too loud when Carl gets home. Dishes are being knocked together in the kitchen sink, and something sounding like Hell's orchestra blares from the living room. Maybe it's always been this loud, he thinks. While the sanding floor wasn't as loud as the rough room, where the wood transformed from solid blocks to recognizable parts of tables and dressers, the whir and hiss of the sanders linger like the memory of a childhood blanket.

He pokes his head in the living room on his way to the kitchen. Doug sits on the couch staring at a cartoon with the volume turned up, his GameBoy on his lap. Carl watches for a few seconds, but he can't understand cartoons anymore. He was raised on Looney Tunes, and then only on Saturday mornings, not this epileptic stuff full of vaguely Asian characters with funny voices and more flashing lights and sounds than a pinball machine. Just looking gives him a headache.

"Finish your homework?"

Doug startles at the sound of his voice. "I will after this show," he says before turning back to the TV.

"You can watch TV after you finish your homework," he says, stepping between his son and the television.

Doug's shoulders fall, and he slides down the couch so he can still see the TV. Rather than play the game of moving around to keep himself in Doug's way, Carl snaps, "Boy!" and Doug stares down into his lap, examining the tiny blank screen in his hand.

"Okay," Doug says.

"What was that?" Carl leans forward, cupping his ear.

"Yes, sir."

Carl straightens and forces a smile. As Doug passes, he reaches out and takes the GameBoy. "Just until you can show me your finished homework," he says.

Doug sulks to his room, and Carl flips the TV off on his way to the kitchen. He sits at the table turning the GameBoy over in his hands. So small and fragile. He can't see what the attraction is. A gizmo probably put together halfway around the world, and not even put together well. Carl twists it in his hands until it bends perceptibly, just a fraction of an inch. He sets it down, afraid he'll wind up breaking something if he's not careful.

"What do kids see in these things?" he asks his wife, who stands at the sink.

Karen turns slowly, her shoulders stiff. "I heard you in there with Doug," she says, focusing on the dishrag in her hands. "I told him he could watch that one show."

"I thought we'd agreed he couldn't watch TV until his homework was done."

She stops twisting the rag and stares hard at him. "No, you decided that. I never said anything of the sort. You can't keep undermining me, Carl." Her arms fall to her sides, but her eyes remain firm.

Carl stares at the table, then picks the GameBoy back up and immediately sets it down again. "I need a shower," he says, ignoring the look Karen gives him as he leaves.

Where You Are From

The announcement was sudden. There had been whispered rumors for years, ever since the textile mills to the east and south of Tucker closed and sent their jobs to Mexico, but no one really expected furniture to follow. Even when Hill-Dale announced the first rounds of layoffs, they were in the cities of Rhyne and Morganton, not Tucker. After all, Hill-Dale Furniture was born in Tucker, *was* Tucker, a small industrial empire built by the Hill and Dale families, who had pooled their resources after the Civil War and thought to become artisans. The story was in every training video, every glossy brochure printed to advertise new product lines. It was one Carl's father never tired of telling.

And it was his father, Lucas, who gave Carl faith in hard work. Carl never knew his grandparents. According to Lucas's reluctant memories, Carl's grandfather was a farmer in name only who drank and womanized when he should've been planting, while his grandmother was a saint, the soft resin that held the family together until she died giving birth to Lucas's brother. The story went that after his wife's death, Carl's grandfather disappeared, claiming that he would come back for his children once he'd settled himself in Detroit. Eventually, the farm was sold to pay off his debts, the younger children were sent to live with an aunt south of Asheville, and Lucas, thought old enough to care for himself at sixteen, left school and moved to town to find work.

Lucas taught his son that this was his true birth, the day he answered an ad calling for janitors at the newly built Hill-Dale Plant #7. Lucas started his working life with his nose down and his mind focused on whatever task the foreman put before him, determined only to not become his father, and the company rewarded him. He only spent a year sweeping sawdust before he was promoted to the varnish room, and by the time he retired Lucas had climbed to Shop Foreman. He taught his son that if a man works hard enough to satisfy those above him, he will in turn be satisfied. And Carl believed. Lucas was living proof.

But then one morning it was over. A meeting was called at the beginning of the shift. And everyone, from the guys on the loading dock to the women in the embroidery room, from the boss-men who worked in the upstairs office to the cleaning ladies who always left the bathrooms smelling like a mixture of pine and bleach, was congregated in the loading lot.

Carl watched from behind his men – he'd been made Supervisor of the sanding room just months before – as J.E. Hill, the great-grandson of founder Wilton and company CEO, stood on the lip of the dock and spoke solemnly about "restructuring" and the "global economy." It was late March, and the air had the knife-blade crispness that cut into lungs and always reminded Carl of high school baseball. After Hill, a lady from the local community college talked about retraining programs and the like before the company's human resources director stepped up and gave them the bare facts: in three months, Hill-Dale Plants 1, 3, and 7 – all in Tucker – would cease operations indefinitely. All full-time employees with at least five years' experience would receive three-months' full salary followed by six months of unemployment benefits at half-salary. Those with less experience would receive half.

Lucas was certain the closings were temporary. He hung on the word *indefinitely*. They would've said permanently if they weren't going to re-open, he said. I know their language. I know what kind of man J.E. Hill is, he said, and he isn't one to leave his workers in the ditch.

Now it's March again. The plants haven't reopened, and the final unemployment check is already spent. Even with Karen's job, it won't be long before the bills start coming on pink paper instead of white. He figures they can make it by on credit cards for a little while, but after that he isn't sure.

When Carl gets out of the shower, Karen is waiting.

"We need to talk," she says, standing by the door between the master bath and bedroom with her arms crossed.

"What about?"

"I'm worried about us."

Carl tugs on a pair of jeans and looks at his wife. She's wearing a pair of sweatpants and an old tank top she bought at Myrtle Beach a few summers back. He remembers them laughing at a street performer, the heat of the sun. He was pale but in shape then from working; he had muscles instead of bones. The day after she bought it, they stood on their balcony and watched the morning sun play across the Atlantic, his arms wrapped solidly around her shoulders from behind.

He'd never lost his attraction for Karen the way most of the men he'd worked with did with their wives. Unlike the doughy creatures with bad perms and saddle pants he'd seen bringing forgotten lunches and the like to the plant, Karen had taken the softness of womanhood gracefully. After Doug was born, her breasts settled rather than sagged, and her stomach softened instead of spread. He especially loves how her hair, neither blond nor brown, surrounds her face, the ends turning inward below her chin so they frame her smooth features like an old-fashioned portrait.

"Why are you worried?" he asks.

"How could I not be?"

He refuses to meet her stare. "Well, don't."

He starts to leave. It's one of the only conversations they have anymore. The content occasionally changes, but it's always Karen lecturing, him explaining, and her not understanding.

"No," she says, beating him to the door and closing it. "This is what I'm talking about. You can't just run off whenever I bring something up you don't feel like talking about." Her eyes are a cold green, tinged with flecks of fire that threaten to escape.

He leans against the wall. "Okay, then talk."

"You can't keep undermining me, Carl. You can't just keep ignoring my opinions."

"What opinions do I ignore?"

"You're kidding. You've got to be," she laughs purposefully. "Like this afternoon with Doug. I told him he could watch that one show."

"The boy needs to do his homework, Karen," he interrupts.

"Like you even know what homework he has." She steps towards him. "When was the last time you actually *talked* to your son, Carl? When was the last time you knew anything about him?"

"What is there to know?" he asks, not bothering to keep his voice too low. "He doesn't do anything but sit around the house and watch TV or play those stupid video games." He steps away from the wall and starts to pace. "What? You want me to take him fishing? Is that it?"

Karen stalks across the room, stopping only when their faces are inches apart. Carl could headbutt her, she's so close. "Goddamnit, keep your voice down. You want him to hear you say that shit?"

"Seriously, Karen," he says, the words coming out ragged like planks of wood after the first rough cut of a saw, "I don't know what to do with him. He hated basketball. He quit the scouts after two months. He hasn't shown an interest in anything."

She takes a step back. "He isn't interested in anything you're interested in, but that doesn't mean he doesn't have interests."

"Like what?"

"Anime."

"What the fuck is that?" he asks.

"The cartoon he was watching?" she points in the direction of the living room, her arm as sharp as a sword. "It's from Japan, and it's called Anime. He wants to be a cartoonist, Carl."

"How do you know that?" he asks.

"I talk to him; it's not like it's a secret."

A cartoonist. He stares beyond Karen at the bed's headboard, becomes lost in it. The intricately carved loops, the posts crafted to look like columns. He'd bought it at a company auction the Christmas before last as a present to Karen. It had been the first product line he'd overseen after his promotion to Supervisor: Aegean Villa. It had been nearly impossible to sand; each piece had to be sanded with the delicate hand flutter to create the illusion of six sharp grooves while dulling the edge enough to be safe. He'd been so proud of it, and the line had sold well, keeping the plant busy, filling orders from distributors as far away as Italy.

"He wants to draw. For a living," Carl says. He speaks slowly so there's no misunderstanding.

"Yes, he does." Karen looks at him like he just exposed himself as an idiot. "He's actually really good, too. His teacher says he could study art in college. There are schools for that now," she says, her voice lowering. "You'd know that if you ever made it to one of his parent-teacher conferences."

"College," Carl says. "You think the boy should go to college to learn to draw?"

"If he wants to when he gets to be that age, yes."

"If he wants to? We shouldn't have any say in that?"

Carl starts to pace again, his legs taking off towards the dresser without him consciously ordering them to. He picks up a small wooden heart leaned against the back wall that Doug had made in shop class for their anniversary. Thank God shop is still a required class.

"We need to encourage him, Carl."

Karen's eyes have become rigid. Carl is reminded of volcanic rock, smooth and cool to the touch. It's probably the steam from his shower thinning, but even the room feels a few degrees cooler. He turns the varnished heart over in his hand, remembering how impressed Doug had been when Carl had known it was pine just by the weight in his hand. Too light for maple or oak, he'd told his son.

"What about preparing him for the real world?" Carl asks. "If he's going to college to draw, he should study drafting. Be an engineer. Otherwise it'd just be a big waste of money."

"An engineer doing what? Drawing unemployment?" Karen asks.

"There's still a market for engineers. Hill-Dale hasn't gone out of business, Karen. They're still here." He stops pacing and sets the heart back down. Doug had done a good job burning his and Karen's names into the wood with lettering so fancy it looks like it belongs in a dusty book somewhere. He'd make a good engineer, Carl thinks.

Karen's lips move, but Carl can't hear what she's said. Still, he's pretty sure he understands. "What was that?" he asks.

"For now," Karen repeats in her full speaking voice. She stares straight at him, daring him to face her. He can't.

"I know you don't think the plant's going to reopen," he says. "But I wish you would trust me. Operations are still *suspended*; no one's mentioned ending for good."

"What if they do?" Karen interrupts. "What if it is gone for good?"

Carl takes a seat on the end of the bed, feeling his knees under the thin denim. They feel bigger, and he can't tell if it's because his knees have swollen or his legs have shrunk. "It can't be. Lucas says—" he starts before Karen cuts him off again.

"I know what your father says, but the world's changed."

Karen stands over him. She must see something in his face, some weariness or fear, because her eyes soften, become slightly wider. "What about retraining at the community college?" she asks.

Carl laughs. "Retraining to do what? Bobby Harris went through that as soon as the plant shut down, and it didn't do him a damn bit of good." Bobby had worked under him, manning the kickback sander where Carl himself had started. Younger and in better shape, Bobby eventually gave up and joined the Army after the attacks in September. Now he's in the desert somewhere waiting to go into Iraq. Carl knows that if a young man like Bobby couldn't find work, there isn't a chance in hell for him, or for any of the others. "Besides, the plant is what I know," he says. "It's what I'm good at."

Karen opens her mouth, then closes it without speaking. She twists the ring on her finger like she's tuning an old radio.

The alarm is off when Carl wakes up the next morning, the bed empty and house quiet. The clock reads 8:07. If the plant were still open, he'd be nearly forty-five minutes late for work.

He makes his way to the kitchen and turns the coffee maker back on to heat the congealing liquid Karen left in the bottom of the pot. There's a note from her on the table, weighed down by her empty mug. It's brusque: *Working a double to make up for yesterday. Pick Doug up from school. – K.*

He burns some toast and eats it dry, staring out the window. It's sunny, and hints of green are starting to show on the trees outside even though it's too early for the first birds to start appearing. He hates the daytime.

After dressing and cleaning up the kitchen from breakfast, he's at a loss. In the end, after glancing through the paper to make sure nothing interesting is happening that he could be a part of, he decides to drive out to his father's house.

After Carl's mother's death, Lucas refused any idea of going into a retirement home and instead bought a house in the rolling hills south of Tucker. Away from town, a smattering of houses sit among large tracts of pastureland leading down to the Catawba River. It's a beautiful drive on two lane roads with faded yellow lines, miles away from the single highway crowded with furniture outlet stores and fish camps that connects Tucker to Rhyne, but Carl barely notices. When he'd left the house, visiting Lucas had been just an excuse for getting out of the house. But the closer he gets, the more he needs to talk with his father.

Carl's memories of his father from childhood are of brawn, a man who stood a foot taller than most of the men he knew. When Carl was four or five, before he started school, Lucas had taken him to work for the first time. Lucas hadn't even slowed as he carried Carl down the line to make sure all the men were introduced while dodging pallets of untreated pieces and the sprayers' hydraulic cables. At one point, Carl thinks his father picked up a bed's headboard that was leaning against a pole with his free arm and put it back once they'd passed, but he's willing to admit that the headboard lifting may or may not have happened on that visit. What he remembers clearly, though, is having to lean down from Lucas' chest to shake the gloved hands of the men, how he could see the tops of their heads, how small and insignificant they appeared next to his father.

It was the same at home, too, where both Carl and his mother seemed to exist solely as extensions of Lucas' immensity. Carl remembers how he'd start listening for Lucas' boots on the porch the moment he heard the plant's whistle, how he looked forward to seeing his father's shape fill the doorway like a king returning home from battle. During the day, Carl's mother was the steward of the house, but after three-thirty, it was always Lucas who spoke for the both of them, always Lucas who had the final word.

Lucas meets Carl on the porch, a stooped figure so eroded by time and failing lungs that his skin is draped off his skeleton like sheets over furniture. Carl hugs his father lightly, careful not to squeeze the old man too hard, and they shuffle inside to the easy chair where Lucas's canister of oxygen waits.

"So, what brings you by?" Lucas says, his voice little more than a rasp until he can fit the nose piece on correctly and start the flow of gas.

"Nothing much, really."

They go through the requisite small talk while Carl looks around the den. Most of the objects from the old house are here, relics from Carl's childhood. The appliances – the television, a VCR Lucas bought sometime in the '80's, a digital clock with oversized numbers – are new, but the furniture, with only one or two exceptions, is the same. He sits on the old couch, its olive leather now covered by a thin sheet of plastic.

"Karen worrying you again?" his father asks, his voice strengthened by the oxygen.

Carl sighs, stares at the muted television where the Weather Channel shows pictures of a snowstorm in the Midwest. Cars slide across straight, flat roads while a man in a blue hooded jacket silently mouths words at the camera.

"I guess so. She got on me last night pretty bad."

Lucas grunts, "Well, I can sympathize. Now, you know I don't blame you, son, but it's hard on a woman when her man is out of work."

Carl stares down at the coffee table. He focuses on a scratch, barely perceptible, that he'd put on the corner playing with his Matchbox cars over forty years before, thinking of how easy it would be to sand it out and refinish the whole thing. Make it look nice again.

"Hard on me too, Pop," Carl says, then lower. "I don't know that she believes me anymore."

"Well, it can't be too much longer," Lucas pauses to cough in huge racking heaves that go on for almost half a minute. When he finishes, it takes him a few deep breaths of oxygen before he can continue. "I'm surprised it's been this long. Hell, part of me still can't believe they shut down at all. I tell you, son, it's not my world anymore. My time has passed. I know this, though," Lucas continues. "You've got to have faith. If you have that, she'll respect you even if she don't agree with you. The fighting doesn't matter, either, as long as she respects you as the man. That's what's important."

Carl looks away. "Last night it was about Doug," he says.

"What? The fight? Boy getting in trouble at school?" Lucas asks, reaching down to fiddle with the canister.

Carl knows he doesn't have too much more time. Once Lucas opens the valve to a certain point it's only a matter of time before he falls asleep in his chair, his lungs scrubbed clean enough for his body to rest. "No, it's not that," he pauses, unsure how much he should tell. "She's been encouraging these fancy notions he gets in his head instead of preparing him for the real world."

Lucas turns back to the TV and mumbles something. "What kind of notions?" he asks after a minute.

"Japanese cartoons. They have some kind of name I can't remember. Thinks he's going to grow up and have someone pay him to draw all day."

Lucas laughs, sending him into a coughing fit so bad Carl runs to the kitchen and comes back with a glass of water. After a few sips Lucas can breathe again.

"Aw, hell," he manages, "he'll grow out of that soon enough."

"You think?"

"I know. When you were his age, you thought you were going to be a ball player." He laughs again, this time able to keep himself from coughing. But when he looks at Carl again, his eyes have taken on the unfocused sheen of the blind. "All it took was time. Just take an interest without being too encouraging. Take him out with you; show him how to act like a man, and he'll straighten himself out. There ain't a woman who can show him that." Lucas leans back, chuckles quietly to himself. "But, boy, you had it bad. I took you to work once and you spent the whole day wearing that glove of yours. Remember that glove, son? It still around anywhere?"

"I don't know, Pop," Carl says, standing and getting an afghan from the hall closet. He can recall the glove, but not that particular trip to the factory. But as he thinks about it, he gets a hazy recollection. He *had* thought he'd be a ball player, kept at it through four years of Legion ball during high school. But then the real world had come calling and all that had been put aside. Somehow the thought is comforting.

By the time he returns to the den Lucas is asleep. Carl drapes the afghan over his father, allowing his hand to linger on the old man's shoulder for just a minute before he lets himself out of the house, making sure to lock the door behind him.

It's not quite time for lunch when Carl gets close to town, merging onto the nearly deserted Westside Highway that stretches between the old Hill-Dale plants and 321. There are still three hours to kill before he's supposed to pick Doug up from school, and Lucas' advice echoes in his head. When he comes to the turnoff for his neighborhood, he doesn't take it.

Something's different when he pulls onto the gravel, outer parking lot, though it takes a few moments before his brain registers exactly what it is. The gate is open. Carl has to stop the truck, breathe deep. It's the same nervousness he felt the first day he'd driven through the gate as an employee, a mixture of shock and terror, the feeling deep in the gut that here is where your life pivots and you either succeed and make your way or fail miserably and publicly. He puts the truck back into gear and slowly passes the empty gate house.

He drives around to the loading dock. Three Hill-Dale trucks are there with men coming in and out of the open loading bay. The trucks are pickups, big commercial models with extended beds and doubled tires on the back wheels. Dulled white paint with the distinct Hill-Dale logo and its Victorian lettering stenciled on the doors. Carl parks with the grill of his truck facing them and gets out.

"Sir? Sir!" An older man wearing a hard hat has walked up to Carl without him noticing. "Can I help you?" he asks.

Carl opens his mouth, but nothing comes out. He can't take his eyes off the open bay door, remembering it when it bustled with shipments going out, seeing the image of J.E. Hill silhouetted against it that awful day.

"I'm sorry, sir, but authorized personnel only," the man says after a minute. The voice isn't familiar and neither is the face, but Carl feels like he knows him. Short and stocky with a salt and pepper mustache and narrow, precise eyes; this was the type of man he'd worked among all those years. He knows how to talk to them.

"I was a supervisor here in the sanding room," he says, forcing a brusque confidence into his voice. It's the voice of men talking to men.

"Oh, just came to check up on what we're doing?" the man asks, relaxing. Hispanic men carry toolboxes into the plant, and the man turns to shout some Spanish word at them. "Well, nothing much today. I'm just heading up this crew getting ready for them to come down and take all that old equipment out." He nods towards the door, where two men come out carrying an old electrical switchboard between them. "You know, pulling the electric, loosening the bolts, that kind of work."

"They going to refurbish the place?" he asks.

"Wouldn't know about that. All I know is that I'm supposed to get these guys," he interrupts himself to shout more instructions at the men who'd carried the switchboard out, now standing by the bed of one of the trucks. "Sorry," he says, turning back to Carl. "These goddamned Mexicans. I swear, the way things are going we'll all be talking Spanish before too long."

Carl watches the men walk slowly back to the loading dock, their thin arms swinging like inmates tied to a chain-gang. He wonders how much Hill-Dale pays them. "Well, the old place could damn well use refurbishing," Carl says.

"Maybe," the man shrugs. "Anyway, like I was saying. We're just finishing up here, and this afternoon we're supposed to go over and ready numbers one and three. Next week the big trucks are going to come in and pull it all out. After that, I don't have a clue." The man turns and spits.

Carl thanks him and turns to leave. He watches the men for a few more minutes before he cranks the old Ford and points it towards the front gate. He knows what he must show his son.

The secretary isn't happy, but Carl remains insistent.

"It's the second day in a row Doug's been taken out early," she repeats, although he can see that she's writing out the release note as she speaks. "We're just worried that he'll get behind if this keeps up."

"I'll make sure he keeps up with his work." He glances around the office. He always feels uncomfortable in places like this, rooms with short, scruffy carpet and cheap particleboard furniture. They make him feel dirty. He glances down at his hands, conscious of every speck and smudge the fluorescent bulbs bring out.

The secretary, by comparison, is spotless but ugly. She's wearing a floral dress with one of those white lace collars that bring tea parties to mind, and her hair is nearly a crime in itself, a perm sprayed into place inches above the woman's round face. But there are no blemishes, and each freckle on her arm stands out like it's supposed to be there. She wears a simple gold band on her ring finger, and Carl wonders what kind of man could honestly call himself happily married to such a woman.

She pauses and glances up at him, "What's the reason?" she asks.

"Educational experience," he smirks, proud of himself for making the secretary's eyes narrow with anger. She thrusts the sheet at him and points to where he has to sign, and Carl takes a seat in one of the chairs against the wall while he waits for Doug to be paged.

"Hey Dad, what's wrong?" Doug appears by his side, his plain black backpack on his shoulders like a watermelon-sized tumor.

Carl smiles, "Nothing's wrong, son. Just got something to show you."

He leads Doug out of the school and to the truck. "Where are we going?" Doug asks.

"I want to show you what your Pop does," Carl replies. He's trying his best to be friendly, open.

"Mr. Miller's going to be mad at me for missing two days in a row." As they pull out of the parking lot, Carl catches Doug watching the school fade away like a man being taken from his home.

"Cheer up, Doug," he says, giving the boy's arm a playful tap, "Isn't hanging out with your old man better than Mr. Miller's class?"

"I guess."

"What class is it, anyway?"

"English."

Carl barks out a laugh. "Oh, come on," he smiles. "In a few years we'll all be talking in Spanish, anyway."

"I guess," is all Doug manages.

Carl didn't expect it to be so hard. He'd imagined Doug bounding into the truck, some good-natured ribbing back and forth, but his son almost seems frightened of him. He leans against his door watching Carl like he expects him to do something crazy. Although Doug mostly resembles Carl, his eyes came directly from Karen. They have the same cool, jade sheen, the same flecks of fire.

"What?" Carl asks.

"Are you sure you're okay, Dad?"

"I feel fine, son," he laughs again to prove it. "Besides, I thought you were more interested in Japanese cartoons than English, anyway."

Doug's eyes widen for a second, but he quickly recovers. "I just want to get a good grade," he says.

"Well, I understand that," Carl pauses to think of the appropriate thing to say. "But I have faith in you, son. You're a smart one."

"Really?"

"Oh yeah," Carl says, trying to think of an example. "Like that Any May stuff you like. At your age, that would've been way over my head."

"They're just cartoons."

Doug shrugs, but Carl thinks he sees the tiniest fraction of a smile and smiles in turn. "One day I'd like to learn Japanese so I could read the manga, though," Doug says.

Carl nods and murmurs some kind of assent, though he has no idea what his son is talking about. He glances across the seat as they pass through downtown, trying to see if Doug was trying to show him up, but the boy is staring out the window at the town square where a group of men pass around a brown paper bag, sitting around the fountain. Carl is afraid to look. Last week he'd seen a face he recognized among them.

"What were those men doing?" Doug asks once they pass through downtown's southern edge.

"Loitering."

Carl passes their street, its familiar green sign just another in a progression of streets lined with houses built by Hill-Dale back when the company provided housing for its employees as part of the deal, his foot resting a hair more weight on the gas pedal. He senses that his window is closing, and he wants to get to the plant before he loses his son to cartoon daydreams and made-up words.

"Where are we going?" Doug asks as they pull onto the highway, his hand on the door handle.

"Where does it look like?" Carl smiles again as he pulls the truck into the gravel lot. The Hill-Dale men are gone, the gate locked behind them, but Carl remembers that the east side of the fence is missing a section from where a storm had knocked it down years before.

"I thought we were going home."

Carl opens his door and steps out. Doug stays inside the cab, clutching his backpack to his chest.

"Come on," he says to his son.

"Are we even supposed to be here?" Doug reaches down and puts his hand on the handle but doesn't open the door.

"It doesn't matter. Besides, in six months I'll be able to bring you back to see your old man at work." He forces himself to keep smiling until the boy finally opens the door and gets out.

"Really?" Doug asks, making his way around the front of the truck. "They called you?"

Carl starts walking along the fence, giving his son no choice but to follow. "Not yet, but they will. A crew was here this morning getting ready to strip the place so they can get it back up and running."

"You sure that's what they were doing?" Doug asks.

"Sure, I'm sure. I talked to the man myself," he says, reaching out and wrapping his arm around Doug's shoulder. He leads the boy around the corner, into the tall grass out of sight of the highway.

"What did the man say?" Doug stops without warning, and Carl's arm slips to his side. "Was it the manager?"

Carl looks his son over to see if he's mocking him. Kids today are smarter than they were in his day, he thinks, always trying to figure things out on their own.

"He was just a foreman, Doug. And he didn't know too much, but he said there was another crew coming next week," Carl starts walking again.

"How do you know they're going to reopen the place?" Doug asks, catching up. "I heard a kid at school say all the jobs were going to Mexico. That his daddy said the Hills sold us all out."

"Well, they're wrong," Carl snaps. The words sound loud in his head, but they're swallowed by the open air. "I've been working here since before you were born. I know what I'm talking about." He looks over and stares hard at Doug. The boy's eyes meet his only for a moment before turning away. Faith, Carl thinks, he's got to teach the boy to have faith in what a father says.

They reach the gap. From here the plant's intake bays are only a hundred-and-fifty-foot walk across the empty space where the pallets of rough wood were stacked. Carl steps through. On the other side, he waits for Doug to do the same, but the boy wavers just outside, glancing up and down the fence line like he's looking for a back way out.

"There's a No Trespassing sign, Dad," Doug says, pointing further down to where the fence resumes.

Carl reaches back through the gap and tugs Doug through by the hand. He's amazed at how big his son's hand is, thinner, but almost as big as his own.

"Never mind that," he says a little gruffer than he'd intended.

They walk across the lot, the intake bays growing larger and more imposing as they do. Carl is struck by the quiet. This is normally the loudest part of the factory, where the screams of the sawblades as they first meet the raw wood echo across the lot. Instead, one of the first birds of the spring calls from one of the building's eves, a chirping that sounds almost smothered by the silent air. He turns to tell Doug, but the boy doesn't seem to be listening. Instead, he stares at the plant like he suspects an ambush, his shoulders hunched forward and his hands stuffed deep in the pockets of his jeans.

"Are you *sure* this is okay?" Doug asks.

"I've told you, son. I know what I'm doing." Carl tries the door to the right of the bays, but it's locked. He lets go of Doug for a second and steps over to the bay door, testing it with both hands. The steel gives a little, and he's able to lift it open about three feet before something catches. The dark, musty air inside the factory seeps through the crack and Carl breathes deeply, his heart beginning to race. He's missed the smell of the plant's air, thick with sawdust and oil. "Come on," he says, waving for Doug to join him.

"I don't want to be here, Dad," Doug says. Carl takes his son's wrist in his hand and drags him towards the partially open bay. It'll be worth it once they're inside.

"Of course you do," Carl says as he ducks under the door, pulling his son into the darkness with him. "This is going to be yours someday, after all."

Those Who Help Themselves

She'll be back.

I stare at the clock, waiting for the minute hand to lurch forward again. The clock says it's almost 8:00, and I don't know if I've been asleep or how long I've been asleep for. Easy to lose track of, unlike a girlfriend.

She's only been gone a week, I remind myself. She's done this before and never takes it too far. Her mother will say something to piss her off, and she'll be back.

It's not her I miss, anyway. It's April. I've told Theresa before, *you have every right to hate me, but don't you keep April from me. Don't you fucking dare.*

I turn on the TV and reach for the bottle by the couch. There's an infomercial on for a food dehydrator, one of those cylinders where you put slices of fruit or meat and they come out completely dry and shrunken in an hour. It looks interesting, and as the alcohol starts to soothe my blood I think about calling the 800-number but don't.

§

"Jesus Christ, Mark. You look like hell."

I want to tell him to shut the fuck up and mind his business.

"Long night, Mr. Mitchell, but I'm fine."

I meet his eye as best I can, reminding myself that half the employees here are high on any given day. Still, Curt said he heard Mitchell and one of the other geniuses who made their way up the Wal-Mart ladder talking about firing me last week. You never know. He's lucky I showed up at all today. It'd been lucky that I needed to piss and happened to see the calendar in the hall on my way.

Mitchell assigns me to stock automotive, which is perfect. It's easy to sneak out to the loading dock from there.

Curt comes out during his morning break. I'm feeling like absolute hell, squatting against the back wall with my forehead on my knees, waiting for the slug I'd just taken from the flask to calm my blood a little.

"Damn. It's on you bad today." He smiles, showing the gap where his left canine once was. Curt's an ugly fucker – his face looks like a belt sander was taken to it – and he's at least forty, but he's my best and only friend on the job. Besides, he's a great connection.

"Still upset over that bitch?" he asks, lighting a cigarette and offering me one.

"It's my kid I'm pissed about."

"You tried to see her?"

The alcohol is working, but not quite fast enough. In a minute, I'll have to go back inside before Mitchell or one of his assistants misses me, and I'm still itchy. I reach in my pocket for another swig.

Curt shakes his head. "Might want to ease off that," he says, straightening a leg and pulling something from his pocket. "Here. This will fix you up."

In his hand, wrapped in a plastic bag, is a small glass pipe streaked with residue and God knows what all else. In its mouth is a small white rock. Meth, probably.

I hesitate. It's not like I haven't used some over the years, but this still feels like a transgression. I've been drunk at work a lot, but this is something else.

"Want to make it through the rest of your shift?" Curt asks.

I watch a crow drag a piece of cut zip tie across the back lot and feel my skin crawl. Another shot or two would fix that, but I'd probably start slurring my words. When I think about the rest of the shift, it stretches out in front of me like a two-lane through a desert, no end in sight. So I take the pipe.

"Sir? Are you okay?"

There's a customer in my face. Some old hag with huge rose-hued glasses and a dye job to match. It looks like she stole Ronald McDonald's wig, and that thought makes me laugh a little. I'm standing in toys, where Mitchell sent me after I finished in automotive, a full pallet and two open boxes of Muppets at my feet.

"Fine, Ma'am."

I'm flying, and for the first time in what feels like forever, Mitchell isn't pissed at me. He even smiled once I'd finished automotive, and said I could leave early after I finished stocking toys.

"You just seem to be shaking a lot. You got the palsy?"

She reaches out and takes hold of my left biceps, wrapping her bony fingers around the strings of muscle there.

"I've got a granddaughter that's got it. Lord, how she shakes," she says.

"Sorry to hear that."

I try to escape, to cautiously step back and away, but the more I resist the tighter the old crow's grip becomes. I take a step back and accidentally step on an Elmo doll. It starts chattering mechanically in a way that cuts to my bones. She leans a little closer, and I can't help but notice how two silver hairs curl out of her right nostril, wrapping around each other like fighting snakes.

"Young man, are you sure you're okay? You're sweating."

Her breath reeks of mothballs, pungent.

"Goddmanit. I told you I was fine."

I yank my arm free, and she stumbles back like I smacked her, her eyes and mouth forming three perfect 'O's.'

Where You Are From

§

Theresa still isn't back when I wake up. I don't have a clue what time or day it is; I just know I'm alone in the apartment. It has that calm. I'm on the couch, and there's light pouring through the shades. My head feels like hell, parched and brittle. And I'm hungry. Surprisingly, though, the itch is only a dull tickle

In the kitchen, there's a half-drunk two liter of Sun Drop in the fridge, so I grab one of Theresa's coffee mugs from the counter, pour three fingers from the bottle on the table into it, then fill the rest with the Sun Drop to work the kinks out of my arms and legs, clear the fog from my head.

The red light on the answering machine won't stop blinking. I try to count the number of messages but lose track after seven or so. I was at work on Tuesday, so that would make this Wednesday. Or Thursday. I've lost days before, but the thought never quite sits right.

Once I finish the first mug of whiskey and Sun Drop, I sit down at the table and pour another. There isn't anything to eat in the place – I checked. A half-gallon of milk a week past the expiration, a box of baking soda, and a leftover bottle of formula is all that's in the refrigerator. But, the more sips I take, the more my hunger eases, so I sit a minute in the silence, sipping to muster the energy to check the answering machine.

The messages are a waste of time. Calls for Theresa. God knows how many terse messages from collection agencies. A call from Mom that begins, *Pick up, Son. Please* ... Then, at the end of the tape: *Mark, it's Mr. Mitchell down here at the store. Just calling to see where you are. It's Thursday morning, and you were scheduled to come in about two hours ago. Call as soon as you get this.*

Fuck. I look at the clock on the stove and hope the green numbers are figments of my imagination. Four-thirteen. Still no sign of Theresa or April. I light a cigarette and pour another splash of whiskey into the mug, but not too much. I'm going to have to leave the apartment before long.

"The fuck are you doing here? If Mitchell catches you here after your no-call/no-show, you're fucking gone."

Curt leans across the sporting goods counter, his elbows obscuring the display of knives and boxes of cartridges for the rifles lining the wall behind him. He glances side-to-side as if Mitchell were a demon who could be summoned by name. Curt's right – I shouldn't have come – but after leaving the apartment and stopping by the ABC store there really wasn't much else I needed to do but see if I couldn't find Theresa at her mama's, and there's not much more I dread than dealing with Theresa's mother. She's always been crazy, but since all the problems started between me and Theresa, she looks at me in a way I feel in my spine, like we're kin in some way. The thought of facing her just for the chance to talk to Theresa and see April got to me, and I found myself in the parking lot of Wal-Mart. Then I got to thinking about how much that little taste Curt gave me the other day had helped, and that led me inside.

Curt nods as I explain all this, still looking around like he expects Mitchell to jump out of the box of basketballs beside the counter or drop from the ceiling. When I finish, he looks at me and grins.

"Boy, you've caught the itch, ain't you?" he asks.

"Don't fuck with me."

He glances around again, watching until an old man who had been pawing through a rack of fishing lures finds what he is looking for and disappears down the aisle then digs in his pocket, pulling out another little cellophane pouch and holding it down by his hip behind the counter.

"You got your smokes on you?"

I nod, confused, and fumble for them. I'm suddenly nervous, the image of Mitchell catching me now flashing through my head.

"Good," Curt pulls a small rock from the bag and sets it on the counter next to a pen holder by the register. "Stick that in one of your cigarettes for when you get outside. If you want more, stop by the house later. I got to keep the rest to get me through the rest of today." He breaks into a smile, and I feel comfort. "One of my worthless fucking coworkers didn't show up today, so it's going to be a long shift," he laughs.

"Is Theresa here?"

I'm standing on the front porch of the house Theresa grew up in and where she was living when we first started dating, but her car isn't in the driveway. Still, I figured it was worth the shot. I want another cigarette, hoping for some residual taste. Psychosomatic, even. I don't care.

"Mark, you've got a lot of nerve showing up here."

I'm feeling alright, though. Ready to play nice.

"I know. I do. But, Ms. Coffey, you've got to know how sorry I am."

"She had bruises, Mark. *Bruises.*"

That word stings. But it's not true. I would remember something like that.

Ms. Coffey crosses her bony arms. She looks like Theresa would if you put Theresa in one of those food dehydrators for too long. I keep trying to peek around her, hoping for a glimpse of April: a car seat, a playpen, but it's too dark in the living room. Or it's too bright outside.

"Is April here?" I ask.

She leans over, putting her face inches from mine so I can smell the dust from her clothes. Up close, her eyes are the spitting image of her daughter's, right down to the flakes of amber scattered across the green of her irises like tears.

"Mark, are you … high on something?" she asks. It's almost as if she's surprised.

"Of course not." I fake shock, but her question gets to me. Like she has some room to judge, living like a shut-in out in Lord's Creek miles away from town in a house built God-knows-when. It was a shithole when Theresa still lived in it. And it's probably not safe for April now. The porch is missing some of its floorboards, and there probably aren't three flakes of paint left on the entire thing. I decide then that when I get April back in my arms there's no way I'm ever letting her come back here.

Ms. Coffey shakes her head and runs a hand through her tattered perm. "Well, Theresa took off with her somewhere, and I don't know when they'll be back." She takes a step backwards, off the porch and back into the living room.

"Will you tell Theresa to call me at least?"

The door closes without a response, and I'm left standing on the porch steps alone.

When I get home, I know Theresa has been here. I can feel it. Something in the air, either perfume or baby powder. I stupidly call her name but get no reply.

I check the house. The nursery has been stripped. The crib, the changing table, the extra baby carrier and car seat – all gone. Stuff I paid for. I stand there for a second before I think to check the money. I keep it in an old *Doral* cigarette tin hidden behind some old t-shirts in my dresser, nearly a thousand dollars that I've squirreled away here and there over the years and only dipped into when I was desperate.

When I open it, though, all that's inside is a ten-dollar bill and a folded note, and for a second I think my legs will collapse. I make my way back to the kitchen where I'd left the bottle of Old Mill Stream and sit down to read the letter. Most of it is bullshit – whining over how much I've changed and shit like that – but at the end of the letter she'd written: *I can't keep pretending April is safe around you. We're not coming back. Please don't try to find us.*

I pour another good shot of whiskey and swallow it, thinking. She's threatened to leave for good plenty of times before, but she's never written it down. And she's never, ever taken all April's stuff with her. I pour another shot. Then another. The thought of going through the days without April to think about makes my shoulders tense, like someone is tightening a screw between them. I think about how fucked up Theresa is to think she can keep my daughter from me and start to get worked up. Then the shots start easing the tension a little, and a plan starts to come together in my head.

"Hey Mark. What's up?"

Curt looks surprised, and his voice is wary, like I caught him jacking off. But he's the one who told me to stop by.

"You busy?"

"Nothing too important," he says, not answering the question but opening the door enough to let me inside.

I've never actually been inside Curt's house before. The closest I've come is dropping him off after work before he bought his truck. I'm amazed at how much shit he has. A brand-new big screen TV sits against one wall, and cords run from it to a refrigerator-sized stereo cabinet set up in the corner. All in a tiny, clapboard mill house in West Tucker.

"Jesus Christ."

"Like the set-up?" Curt smiles and picks up a burning cigarette from an already overflowing ashtray. The house smells like him. Thick and polluted.

"Yeah. Nice."

He smirks and takes a bow like some kind of carny. "All courtesy of our good friend Mr. Sam Walton."

"No shit?"

"Yep. Stole every last piece off trucks myself." He throws himself down on a sofa covered by a ragged quilt. "All it took was some creative editing on a few stock reports."

"Nice," I nod my head. I wish I'd been smart enough to think of it and say so. Curt grins. His teeth look especially gray in the smoky room.

"Yeah, it's just something I picked up back while I was hauling freight." He leans over the sofa's arm and returns with a pipe and small jar. "I figure this is why you stopped by," he says. "Though you seem to be about lit up already."

"What are you talking about?"

Curt glances up at me and laughs like I've said something funny. "Shit, you haven't stopped swaying once since you came in and you smell like a goddamned distillery. Sit down before you fall through my coffee table."

I take the recliner next to me, half-embarrassed and half-insulted, and sit with my elbows on my knees. I thought I was maintaining. I *feel* coherent. But I've learned that it's best to not argue. Let people believe whatever they want and you're more likely to get what you want.

"So, what's up?" Curt takes a rock from the baggie and puts it in one end of the pipe, then strikes his lighter and starts dancing the flame along the length until a thick white cloud fills the pipe, which he sucks down in one quick *whhitt* before packing another and handing it to me. The first hit clears my head, and as Curt loads himself another hit, I start to tell him about talking to Theresa's mom while she was at the apartment robbing me blind.

"So, what are you going to do about it?" Curt says when I finish, blowing another near-perfect cloud to the ceiling.

"I was hoping you could help," I say, and start to lay out the plan I'd been formulating since leaving the house. It's not complicated. Theresa has always liked Curt, and I know that if he's with me she'll be more likely to talk, and if I can just get her talking, I can get her to hand me April. Just for a minute, I'll tell her, before bolting. But, the more I talk the more I start to realize it would never work. I don't even need to see Curt's forehead wrinkle, though it does, to hear myself, how stupid I sound. In the end I just trail off, leaving that idea to dissipate among the smoke, and reach for the pipe and bag on the table without even thinking.

Curt leans forward and stops my hand. "You might want to slow down. You aren't used to this, and you're more than halfway gone already," he says, and he's right – I know he's right – but that doesn't stop me from wanting more. It's just like drinking used to feel a long time ago: Good and clarifying, like I'm on the verge of figuring out the answers to all my questions. But I know I could feel even better, have more of the answers if only I had more.

But, it's his house, his drugs, so I stand and begin to pace, which must excite my bladder because all of a sudden I feel like I've swallowed a water balloon.

"You got a bathroom I can use?" I ask.

Curt points down the hall. "Through the bedroom," he says, flipping on the TV and filling the air with canned screams.

The bedroom is trashed. There isn't a bed, just a mattress on the floor covered by an Afghan riddled with cigarette burns. Clothes lay in greasy piles stacked against a particle board dresser so cheap it could only have come from Walmart. The only clean area is in the far corner where a gun case lies open.

I step around a pile of old *Popular Mechanics* and make my way to the case. From the doorway I could see a rifle barrel poking over the lip of the box. The case isn't large – it only has places for two rifles carved into the green felt padding – but it's overflowing. Curt's got a shotgun, two rifles with nickel-plated barrels so shiny they look like polished silver, and two Glocks piled on top of each other like toys in a toy box.

I pick up the pistol on top, a 9mm subcompact according to the lettering on the side. I pull back the slide and a bullet pops out and lands on the mattress. It's loaded. I haven't held a pistol since my dad used to take me shooting in the woods behind our house, but it feels right. Heavy and cold. Much better than having Curt with me. Thinking about dad, one of those stupid sayings they must teach assholes like him in college appears in my mind – *Business 101: How to Run a Business in the South*. First Lesson: The Lord helps those who help themselves, son - and along with it, a new plan. I tuck the pistol into my pants against the small of my back and go piss.

On my way back to the living room I hear Curt flipping through the channels, broken phrase followed by broken phrase. Laughter. A gunshot. I reach around and feel the pistol's grip in the small of my back, trying to look natural as I sit back down in the chair.

"Here. This'll take that edge off."

Curt hands me the pipe. From the look on his face and the sharp smell in the room, it's clear he took a few hits in the time I was gone. He'd apparently settled on a rerun of *The Andy Griffith Show*, and we sit and pass the pipe back and forth as Andy tries to help Barney win his girl over. We laugh, but the more we watch the more it gets to me, watching this Thelma chick string Barney along while Andy plays it for laughs. The more it gets to me, the more I feel the weight of the pistol pressing into the small of my back.

Curt passes the pipe back to me, and after I hit it I say:

"I'm going to kill her."

It just pops out, like I'm seeing how it feels to say. It doesn't feel good, but not bad, either. Messy.

Curt laughs, still watching the TV. "Don't be too hasty," he says.

"I'm not kidding," I say, but I don't know whether I am or not. The gun feels solid against my back, and that feels right.

"Hey." Curt leans forward, and when I hand him the pipe back he tucks it back away along with the baggie. "Seriously. Get a hold of yourself." He's got this junkie's grin on his face, all peaceful and calm like some Arab king surrounded by virgins. "Go home, clean the house, fucking do something to take your mind off things. Jesus," he laughs again and lets himself fall back against the couch.

"Sure thing, man. Whatever."

I shrug, trying to play it cool, but Curt's looking at me.

"Seriously. You're not going to do anything stupid, are you?"

I laugh, and he does too. For the first time I notice that he's moving slower, talking slower, and I wonder if he's already starting to come down. I don't see how that's possible. I'm flying. My skin burns. On fire. Alive.

"Hey, I'm going to get out of here."

I shake hands with Curt and tell him I'll see him at work. He tells me to be careful, asks if I'm going home. I say yes, but I know that's a lie. First, I'm going to talk to Theresa.

Even If

When I first saw the car pull off Mulberry Creek Road and start winding up my driveway, I thought it had to be a sheriff. I never have gotten a lot of unannounced visitors living where I do, especially on a weekday morning. From the front porch all I could see of the car before it vanished under the canopy of trees below was that it was grey and looked official.

I knew it would take a minute or two to make it up the driveway, so I stubbed out the joint I'd just lit and ran inside to turn off the music. My morning class down at the community college had been cancelled, so when I woke up I decided to take the day easy, rolling a joint from the little baggie I liked to keep around and putting The Clash on loud enough to hear from the porch.

I got back outside just in time to see the car emerge from the woods into the clearing by the house. The sun had just made its way above Chestnut Mountain behind me, so I couldn't make out who was in the car through the glare, but I saw I'd been wrong thinking it was a cop. It was a Lexus sedan pulling up beside my Datsun, and from the way the sun reflected off the top, one that had been washed recently. Which, in turn, made me wonder what could be so important that someone would take a car that nice up a half-mile of gravel switchbacks.

"Mr. Fergusson?" The driver called, getting out and standing next to his open door.

I recognized him from somewhere but couldn't quite place him off the top of my head. He looked slick, like some sort of businessman, but he was wearing just a black polo shirt and slacks rather than a suit. I'd learned from years of watching Grandpa deal with everything from poachers to the social workers who'd first brought me to live with him that the best thing to do when someone shows up at your door is to keep quiet and wait for them to tell you their business, so I didn't say anything back, just stood there with my arms crossed and waited.

That seemed to fluster the man; he leaned back into the car for a second before turning back to me. "Excuse me," he spoke again, though without confidence. "I'm looking for Mr. Jackson Fergusson. Is this his address?"

"Yeah, I'm Jackson," I said, stepping down off the porch. "Sorry about that."

He took a few steps forward and we met in front of the car to shake hands. Up close, he looked even fancier. His shirt and pants had creases in them, and when I looked down at the hand I was shaking I saw that each fingernail had been carefully trimmed and filed to look like ten little crescent moons. I felt under-dressed in my t-shirt and jeans and a little put out that the joint would have to wait.

"I didn't mean to just barge in on you like this. Wasn't even sure you'd be home on a Tuesday morning."

He smiled like we'd just shared some sort of joke, but I didn't see any point to smiling back. Whoever the man was, he probably figured that the only reason for a man who wasn't farming to be home on a Tuesday morning was unemployment, and I started to worry that he'd come because of the mortgage being late. I'd had trouble paying since Grandpa died the year before, but the man from Wachovia usually just called and did his best to scare me. Still, it seemed a reasonable next step for them to send somebody in person as a little show of force.

"My class down at the college was canceled."

"A college student, huh?" the man asked, cocking his head and smiling like I'd just performed a magic trick. "What are you studying?"

I was already starting to feel stupid for explaining myself to a stranger on my own property, but I'd brought it up and had no one but myself to blame.

"History, sir."

"What are you planning on doing with that once you get out?"

"Not sure, to be honest. Maybe be a teacher."

"The world always needs more of those. Are you thinking of staying around here or heading out and seeing a bit of the world?" He didn't wait for an answer before continuing, "You know, when I was a young man I traveled to London for a year, and I think it was one of the best experiences of my life ..." He cocked his head while he went on about his travels, tilting his mouth towards me while keeping eye contact. I think I was supposed to feel like he was really telling me something important, but there was something in the look, something in the way the skin around his eyes relaxed just a bit too much for it to be natural, that reminded me of the way a TV preacher stares at the camera just before asking for money.

"I'm sorry," I said when he finished. "But I don't believe we've met before."

He mumbled something about his manners and reached into his pocket, pulling out a business card and handing it across. I had to give it to him, it was an impressive card. The thing was milk-white with the logo for Freeman-McAllister Realtors imprinted real faint into the background, and the name on the card said the man was Jason McAllister in bumps of black letters. After glancing over the card I knew where I recognized him from. His face was on all the billboards around town, the ones that read *Freeman-McAllister Realtors: The Rhyne Metro's Most Trusted Team.*

I waited for him to introduce himself using words, but I guess the card was supposed to be enough because he just stood staring up the ridge behind me like he was trying to figure out how far it was to the top. It seemed like an act designed to make me nervous. I wasn't sure what the bank was trying to pull sending a real estate man up here to talk about London, but it was almost enough to get me blurting something stupid about how we'd been depending on the checks from Grandpa's Social Security until I was out of school, so I guess their plan was working. I thought better of it, though, and kept my mouth shut. No sheriff had come yet, and I knew that a foreclosure had to be done by the law.

After a minute of watching him look around like he was here for some sort of inspection, I decided to break the silence, see if that might make him tip his hand. "I've seen your billboards in town," I said.

"Sorry. It's just such beautiful land up here," he said, turning his attention back to me and pointing to the low ridge opposite the house. "That's all a part of Pisgah, isn't it?"

"From the road on."

Now I knew I was being toyed with. Folks were always telling me how beautiful my land was, especially people who've never lived in the hills and think that the picture on a postcard is all there is to a place. What those people don't understand is that they're right, the land is beautiful, but not for the reasons they think. Grandpa used to tell me that what was significant about the land was the fact that it was ours, and not because we owned a deed but because of the dead we'd planted here, and counting him and my dad we've buried six generations within a two-mile range. The way I see things, if it weren't for that the land would just be land, and in most ways wrinkled land is harder to deal with than flatland. The people who think it's so beautiful up here don't know what it's like to always find yourself in a shadow because the sun spends most of its time behind one ridge or the other, and that only if you're up on one of the slopes. Down on the blacktop, the hills press so close that only the tiniest shards of light break through the canopy like cracks in a cave wall, even in high summer. Those folks have never seen how goddamned ugly the hollow looks after one of the occasional floods. Debris and mud and shit from spilled septic tanks all mixed together, coating the ground and road while the stench of it coats your lungs so that weeks later you still taste it on the back of your tongue every time you sit down to eat. And they've never had to park at the bottom of the driveway in an ice storm, trudging uphill with a backpack and a forty-mile-an-hour wind cutting into your side like a Roman spear. But people don't want to hear that, and, sent by the bank or not, I couldn't see what those things had to do with Mr. McAllister appearing at my front door.

"Now," I said after I'd had a minute to remember my good sense. "You didn't come all the way up here from town just to talk about the view, did you?"

His eyes sharpened for a minute, but then they got soft and he looked at me like I was a little brother being taught the ropes. "No, no," he said, laughing in that forced way that people do. "I came here as a representative for the Westin Group. Are you familiar with them?"

"Like the hotels?"

"Exactly." He sounded surprised. "They don't just own hotels, though. They're also one of the largest chains of luxury resorts in the country, and they've been looking to expand into this area."

I nodded. "They thinking of putting one around here?"

"Well, that's why I'm here." He glanced at his watch. "They're willing to make a very generous offer on your land, Mr. Fergusson. If you have a minute I'd like to step inside to discuss it with you."

I sat on the porch the rest of the morning and into the early afternoon thinking things over. I hadn't felt like doing much since Mr. McAllister left, hadn't even finished the joint I'd rolled or turned back on the music. I was that addled.

It was a fact that my people had lived in these very hills since it was still considered frontier land, free for any brave or dumb enough to try and fight a living out of it, and the house itself was only the second homestead, built by my fourth-generation-back grandfather higher up the ridge to replace the drafty dirt-floor cabin his father had left. He, in turn, had passed forty-three acres that stretched across the crest of

Where You Are From

Chestnut from what was then the turnpike to the narrow strip of fertile bottom-land that ran beside the creek that gave Mulberry its name, down the line until it got to my great-grandfather, who'd split the land in two and gave half to Grandpa and half to his older brother Uncle Raeford when Raeford got back from the Pacific. My grandfather said he'd had enough of farming as a boy, which was why Raeford had gotten the good farming land while Grandpa got the house, so he'd gone down to spend the next forty years before retirement drilling holes for wardrobes and secretaries' joists at the Hill-Dale plants. But he'd kept on living here instead of moving to town, a fact he was proud of. He and Raeford had been raised in this house, and after my father got himself killed during a training exercise down at Cherry Point and my mother started having the breakdowns that drove her back to her people in Avery, he'd raised me here, too.

    Still, when I was a kid I'd figured on moving away the day I turned eighteen. I'd seen the kind of lives my Grandpa and Uncle Raeford lived. Lives tallied by the calluses on their hands, calluses earned through years of working behind machines either indoors or out, and I'd known from a young age that whatever happened I didn't want to spend my life chained to pieces of earth and metal. So to me, life became something that happened on the other side of the ridgeline, in places I'd either seen once or only heard about like Charlotte or New York and Atlanta, places where people went to art galleries and ate in restaurants that had fifty different kinds of coffee and bands like Sonic Youth and Nirvana playing on the stereo. And although I'd never liked school, once I got about halfway through down at Killdary High, I'd figured out that college was the way to go about getting there.

    If my wanderlust hurt Grandpa's feelings, he never showed it. Instead, he'd encouraged me to apply to Blue Ridge State up in Boone even though I knew I didn't have the grades, and when I didn't get in he was the one who took me down to Hopewell Tech to fill out the forms so I could start school there. Hell, he'd even gone so far as to be the one to suggest taking out the mortgage to cover what needs of his and the household Social Security wouldn't, just so I wouldn't have to work while going to school or take any more loans than necessary in my own name. *A young man needs to see the world* was what he'd always say when I'd complain about having to drive thirty minutes just to get to town or the fact that we only got one fuzzy channel on the TV. *The valley will be here waiting,"* he'd say, *Even if I ain't."* Now, a year after the heart attack that killed him, a good chunk of the principal had been used to bury him, and the Social Security checks had stopped coming, but the valley was still here with me in it. And for all my moaning, I'd pretty much come to terms with the idea that I would stay here until I graduated and could pay off the rest of the note. The taxes on the land never came to all that much, so I figured that after the bank was satisfied I could move on and just come back from time to time to check on things. After all, I couldn't imagine this land not being Fergusson land.

If McAllister had his way, though, it wouldn't be for much longer. His briefcase had been full of drawings and maps of the land as it would be, dotted with condos and million-dollar houses leading down the valley to the creek, which itself would become the landscaped centerpiece of a golf course designed by Arnold Palmer. He'd laid the papers out on the living room table one by one, each one more of a desecration than the last. There was even a blueprint for damming the creek at Globe Gap to ward against floods so nobody's "Mountain Getaway," as the brochures called it, would be spoiled. The offer McAllister had handed to me was all typed up on paper every bit as fancy as the business card and just as big as he'd hinted. More than enough to pay off the bank and make a good down payment on a house anywhere in the state, maybe enough to pay for the rest of my college outright.

"Young man," he'd said once he'd finished and sat down across from me in Grandpa's old ladder-backed chair. "I'm not going to lie. You and your uncle are behind enough on your mortgages that the bank is ready to start proceedings."

He'd told me first thing through the door that mine and Raeford's were the only two plots he lacked, but until then I hadn't known Raeford owed a single soul. I did my best not to let my surprise show, leaning back on the sofa and focusing on a knot in the wormwood just above his head.

"I saw in the paper that half the county's in the same boat, and most of the people in the article said they owed more than I do," I'd said. "Why would they go after me first?"

"Economic development. This county's seen its share of trouble lately, and the County Commissioners and Wachovia are both on board to get this deal worked out, get some kind of stimulation back into the local economy." McAllister had smiled as he spoke, but there wasn't any doubt in his voice about the outcome, and one thing I know is that if a man has the gumption to smile as he damns you he ain't bluffing.

I'd nodded, keeping my eyes fixed on the wall behind him. "What if I sold it to someone else? Someone who would lease it to me until I could buy it back."

McAllister leaned over the table to make me put my eyes onto his. They were brown, and I'd realized I hadn't actually noticed them before.

"The truth is, Mr. Fergusson, that no one other than my clients is even interested in this property," he'd said, letting his grin fade into that of a fox the moment before it digs its fangs into your neck. "Now, you could always try to pay off the balance that's past due, but with interest rates going up as they are that wouldn't be easy. Not to mention that if after that the house still fell under foreclosure it would wind up being sold at auction for a loss, and in that case you should realize that you would remain responsible for whatever balance was left after the bank recouped what it could from the sale." He looked at me with the cool sympathy I'd imagine a doctor would have when they told somebody their cancer was inoperable.

"But," he'd continued. "I can't believe that a young man in college wouldn't see this as an opportunity. Surely you never expected to spend your whole life confined to this one little valley? Don't you want out? Don't you want to see some of the world before you're too old?"

"It ain't as simple as all that," I'd said, but I knew McAllister'd seen how much he'd rattled me. Grandpa had mentioned something about still having to pay back the mortgage, even if they took the house, when he'd come home from the signing at the bank, but that had been back when not paying off the mortgage seemed like something that couldn't or wouldn't happen if only because we wished it so. And I guess I'd been wishing it weren't so still.

"I'm sure it's not, Mr. Fergusson. But it is something you should consider very carefully. My clients are dead-set on having this project in full swing by next summer, so before this year is out this deal will have to go through one way or another," he'd said, gathering up his papers and moving to the door, where he ran his hand up and down the hand-planed jamb like he was admiring the handiwork.

I'd nodded from my seat, still looking over the offer I held as if it had a section somewhere telling me what the hell to do, and waited for the sound of gravel under tires to dwindle away.

I stayed outside until evening fell and it got too cold, then went in and turned on the new satellite TV I'd had put in just to get some human voices in the air. But even with the TV's chatter I could still hear the low roar of wind caught in the valley, one of those lonely sounds you only hear when it's absolutely quiet, and I found myself missing Grandpa pretty bad. Other than the new TV and stereo I'd kept the living room as he'd left it. Rows of his almanacs still lined the bookcase, one for each year from 1945 until 2004, and the portrait of a young Mozart sitting at a piano he'd found at a thrift store in Asheville years ago was still hanging above the sofa. Even Grandpa's scent lingered, a mixture of loam and accumulation of years that seemed to seep from the walls and weighted the air like sap, soaked into every corner of the house.

I wondered if Grandpa had ever sat here alone and thought about his own grandfather, a man who'd died when he was still in shirttails. I wondered if he'd ever felt the same burden I felt, the same stagnation. I couldn't imagine the house as anything other than it was, couldn't picture it as ever having been new or with more potential than had already been realized, and no matter how hard I tried I couldn't imagine myself as anything other than I was so long as I stayed. I could've hired a contractor to come in and redo the whole place and it wouldn't make any more difference than me just closing my eyes and pretending when I opened them back up that the old skin of the place had been shed.

I got to concentrating so hard that when I heard footsteps crunching across the gravel I jumped up, feeling like someone had stuck an ice cube down the back of my shirt. I hadn't heard any cars pull up and no headlights had swept across the far wall that I'd seen, but when I opened the door there was Raeford standing at the edge of the porch. He was mid-stride, his hand on the porch rail and his foot hovering above the weathered granite step, and he stared up at me like I'd caught him at something.

"Expecting me?" he asked.

"Wasn't really expecting anybody." Though, when I thought about things, I should've known all along that Raeford would be coming as soon as he'd finished his work for the day.

He grunted and made his way up onto the porch. It was full dusk, and the hollow was mostly dark with only the barest glow rising above the west ridges as a reminder of the sun's existence. In the muted light filtering out through the window shades, Raeford looked like a phantom. He was Grandpa's eldest brother, separated by nearly eight years and two sisters who hadn't made it through polio alive: a long, gaunt shape whose face was only lit where light struck directly, leaving most hidden in shadow.

I asked Raeford inside and made a point to ask how his crop was doing. "I tell you." He stood just inside the door, his hands sitting loosely on his hips. "If it weren't for the subsidy, I'd have starved a long time ago. Brightleaf is supposed to be the hardiest of them, but I'll be damned if it don't take to blight easy enough," he said, looking down at the old wood floor like he was about to spit.

"Can I get you a beer, Ray?" I grabbed the remote off the coffee table and turned off the TV.

"I can't stay but a minute," he said. "I just came to see what you're planning to do."

"About what?" I asked, though I knew. I just didn't want to say it before it was absolutely necessary.

"About this asshole McAllister. I know he come to see you first." Raeford lurched forward a step like he'd just then broken whatever chains were holding him and lifted the offer from where I'd left it lying face down on the couch. "What'd you tell him?"

"Nothing, just that I'd think about it."

Raeford cut his eyes at me, setting his face hard like the stone at a gristmill.

"I don't see what choice I have when it comes down to it, though," I said, but I wasn't able to keep my eyes level with his, so I watched the offer waving in his hand. It looked so out of place against the dark backdrop of the rest of the house, an apple blossom encased in mud.

"Choice? There's always a choice, boy," he said, folding the paper once longways and pressing the crease between his fingers like he was squeezing the moisture out.

"What choice? Try and get up the money and end up losing the house anyway?" I asked, hating the whine in my own voice, the way I fell back into my old way of speaking, like just another hick from Mulberry instead of someone with a little sense and education. "Mr. McAllister is right; there ain't no way I can afford it." It was in my mind to say that he'd told me Raeford couldn't either, but I just couldn't manage to.

I realized then that I'd always been a little afraid of Raeford. He and my late Aunt Virginia hadn't had children of their own, and I'd assumed it was his awkwardness that caused him to talk to Virginia above my head like I wasn't there when I was just a little kid getting babysat while Grandpa was in town, that accounted for the way he would look at me like he thought I was half-crazy if I made even the most offhand comment about the weather after I'd reached puberty. But awkwardness didn't explain the fact that since Grandpa died, I'd hardly seen Raeford and when I did he acted like some crucial part of me was missing, one that led him to always look at me with slanted eyes and to call me "boy" instead of by name, popping his lips like he was clearing his mouth of some stray piece of tobacco each time he said it.

Raeford glanced between me and the sheet still in his hands for a minute, then shook his head again, this time real slow. "There's a big difference between can't and won't," he said almost under his breath.

"What do you mean by that?"

"I mean," he said, looking up and tossing the offer aside like a piece of trash. "That you're saying you'd rather sit up here all day doing nothing than work to keep your own people from being thrown off their land."

"That ain't fair and you know it." It took an effort, but I forced myself to lock eyes with him, to find enough gumption to keep my voice level. My cheeks felt warm but the rest of me felt dangerously cold. "I can't keep my grades up and work enough hours to matter at the same time, and besides, where the hell would I find a job, anyway? The plants Grandpa worked at are gone, Ray, you know that. What would you want me to do?"

"Boy," Raeford said, taking a step towards me and squaring his shoulders. "Let me tell you something. They's always work. I didn't serve no three years in the damn Pacific getting shot to hell by the Japanese for you to stand here and talk to me that way. And your own father didn't go get himself killed in the Marines for it, either. Hell, they's boys dying in Iraq right now, and the Army would sure as hell pay you enough to pay off your debts and then some," he snarled, his lip curling so I could see a part of his long, yellowed teeth. "But you're too good for that, ain't you?"

I felt so cold it was like I was going numb. "Grandpa didn't work all them years for me to go running off with the Army," I said. Easy for Raeford to think I should be willing to fight folk I'd never seen before for his debt, though truth be told I wasn't so sure what Grandpa'd would've wanted me to do. I recalled how much pride he'd taken in keeping the house, how he'd taught me that nothing was more important than the debt we owed to our own blood.

"There's no way he'd of wanted this valley to end up like Boone, either." He shifted his torso, leaning a hair closer without so much as lifting a foot. "Run by rich Yankees from Charlotte who'd just as soon wipe their asses with one of us than look us in the eye."

"I'm not going to argue with you on that," I said. "But we can't stop what happens from happening, Ray, and I can't throw my whole life away for it."

"There you go confusing your 'can't' and 'won't' again," he said, so close I was overwhelmed with his breath, a sickly odor like hot dogs cooked too long. "Won't even discomfort yourself for a few years to save the very house your granddaddy and me was born in, but it don't matter to you, does it?" he asked. "You'll be up there in Boone with them, laughing with the rest of the idiots at me and the other old fools having to sell crap out of shacks on the side of the road in order to eat."

I was so worked up I thought for a second I would faint, but I kept myself steady, my back feeling like a lightning rod storing up electricity while Raeford went on.

"That was your granddaddy's biggest mistake," he said. "Letting you keep those big ideas about college in your head for so long. You got above your raising, forgot what the hell was important so that all you can see are the pretty castles up there at the college. Well, let me tell you something, boy, them castles are as cheap and fake as the ones young'uns put in fishbowls. This here is real, worth a hell of a lot more than some stack of paper notes. And you ain't nothing but a damn coward if you let it get taken. A damn traitor and a coward." He leaned back with his chin in the air like he was daring me to take a swing, and when I didn't he nodded like something had been decided and turned towards the door.

"Uncle Raeford," I managed, although I suddenly felt so squeamish I was afraid I'd be sick if I opened my mouth too far. "Wait a damn second, now." I followed him out onto the porch, barely able to feel my feet underneath me.

"Keep swimming, boy," Raeford called over his shoulder, pausing to spit on the dirt beside his truck. "Like a good goldfish." He laughed once, a sharp bark that lit off the trees and came back to hit me square on, before getting into his truck and driving off, the headlights lighting up the front of the house, casting the shadow of the porch rail across the weathered boards like bars on a cage.

The next morning the house was silent. I walked around in a fog, trying to piece everything back together in my mind. It was good early fall weather, not too cool but on the leading edge of crisp, with a sky dappled by clouds so distinct from the background of blue that they looked like they had to have been painted on, and I found myself sitting on the porch again thinking.

The house faced west, looking down over the lip of trees to the valley's narrow stripe of green and the twin trails of creek and road, one a pale gray and the other a dark crack broken only by flecks of white where the water broke against rocks. Beyond the creek the land rose again, and from where I sat you could watch the opposite hills giving way to the waves of ridges behind, a series of peaks flowing southward towards Asheville, first Grandfather – thin wisps of mist rising from the face like breaths – then Hawksbill and Table Rock and Shortoff with Brown Mountain crouching down in front.

They were all profiles Grandpa had taught me to recognize like some fathers teach sons the distinctions between the tracks and scat of different animals. And it wasn't just the names he'd taught me but the old stories and history, too, blending them together until I couldn't tell the difference between fact and legend. I thought about those nights when he'd sat me on this same porch, on the old pew he'd toted out of Mulberry Baptist when they'd remodeled, and told me how my great-grandfather had talked about hearing *his* father tell of the signal fires the Cherokee lit on top of Table Rock back when we were first clearing the land, fires that announced across the valley that an attack was coming from the whites or Catawbas down by where Rhyne is today. And well before I heard it in school, Grandpa had been the one to tell me that the lights on Brown Mountain that tourists and TV cameras still came to see were the ghosts of slaves who'd escaped their piedmont masters only to become lost forever in the netherworld of our hills. Hills it would take a miracle to save from a future of condos and million-dollar houses.

Raeford was right, I did have a choice in the matter, and these hills did hold everything he and Grandpa had cared for in this world, were everything I'd known of the world. But it wasn't enough.

Strangers All

As she walks out of the Pembroke Funeral Parlor beside her husband, a flash of light near the summit of Killdary Mountain causes Anne to stop at the top of the marble steps, assuming that what she's seeing is an airplane or bird yet somehow knowing it isn't. David stops a few steps ahead and turns at the waist, reminding Anne of a boy who just realized that the dog he was walking is no longer under his feet.

"Anne?" he asks. "You okay?"

"A hang glider."

David walks back with his hands in his pockets. His face is illegible, his eyes obscured behind sunglasses a size too small. They'd fit when he'd first gotten them, but over the past year David had finally begun to match her in the slow deterioration of middle age. His jaws are no longer cut into the sharp ridges they'd been at age forty, and the cleft of his chin is almost completely rounded out, swollen into a soft bulb of flesh.

"I thought they'd torn down the ramp after the crash."

"No. Just put up 'No Jumping' signs. You can see the ramp from the house, David," she says, knowing that the only time her husband goes outside is to mow the front yard, and then only occasionally, the back and sides of the house encased in the woods that spread off Killdary like lichen.

"Well, it's the weather for it, I guess."

"It shouldn't be," she says. Funerals in early March should be cold. The sky slate, the air a scouring pad on the lungs, the ground frozen, maybe even some light rain as a physical token of grief. They should be swathed in fog at least, huddling together for warmth and comfort, hidden. "Not for another month or so at least."

Where You Are From

While the receiving had been open to the public, Anne had requested that the ceremony itself be private, held at the gravesite by the prison chaplain who had seen Mark through his conversion to a religion he'd been raised to doubt and attended by no more than herself and David. Mark's ex-girlfriend Theresa had chosen to separate herself and the child she and Mark had created together – no matter what the court certified, the little girl who was still Anne's only grandchild – from not only Mark, but her and David, too, vanishing so thoroughly that despite Anne's best efforts she hadn't even been able to extend the invitation through a lawyer.

She'd fought, though, fought with every tooth and claw she had for the right to see April, through phone calls and letters and checks for child support that went unanswered and uncashed, the awful consultations with the lawyers where it was explained that in North Carolina, grandparents have no rights for visitation without custody; Anne had even considering filing the paperwork for that crucial custody hearing before David put a stop to it by rightly arguing that April had been through enough without another slog through the legal system. But despite everything she'd never given up. Never.

David rests a hand in the small of her back and applies just enough pressure to let her know they've left the limousine waiting too long, that it's time to go to the cemetery. Around them, Jason and Sharon McAllister shake hands with Linda Maynard while cars start, the handful of other friends who had remained to the end of the receiving busy making their escapes down the hill and into the flow of traffic.

When Mark was a boy, he and Anne would watch the launches together from behind their house, Mark's hand in hers and his eyes open in amazement that the vivid kites had people attached, people who could fly without the aid or security of an airplane. Of course, there had been more of them then, in the craze of the early 1980s when it seemed like every week brought a new crop of amateur stuntmen to the mountain, a trend that had slowly died over the course of the decade until there were only a handful each year. It's been nearly three years since the crash, three years of empty sky until today.

"Anne?"

She turns in her seat. David sits across the compartment from her, bent forward with his elbows on his knees.

"What are you thinking?" he asks, sounding like a high school principal, authoritative but with practiced concern like she's a cracked vase – functional only so long as the pharmaceutical glue holds her broken pieces together.

"Nothing. Just thinking," she says. "You?"

They're stopped at the end of the driveway waiting for a break in traffic. Anne looks for the hang glider, but the limo is facing Killdary and her perspective is limited to one of two essentially similar stretches of Wilkesboro Boulevard. Gas stations, the school bus garage, and the entrance to their neighborhood heading in one direction; gas stations, a grocery store, and the cemetery in the direction of Lord's Creek.

David turns to the window, and for a second he seems to deflate. His shoulders sag; his spine bows like a tree in a storm. She almost reaches out to him, but the moment passes. "I just want this over with," he says as he turns back to face her, his voice once again the calm timbre of forbearance, his eyes still hidden.

That day the police arrived at the door, confirming the fear Anne had felt since seeing the previous day's papers, she'd wanted David to do what he always had in the past – stay strong and take care of the problem with the same austere determination that had once served him so well at work. The day Mark broke his arm while she was trying to teach him to ride his bike, it had been David who rushed home from the bank to drive them to the hospital. While she sobbed in the backseat, David told Mark on the way about how the bone would grow back stronger, turning the situation into a lesson about overcoming hardship in the same voice he used when Mark brought home a "C" on his report card or missed the game-winning shot. When she had the wreck driving them home from some party or another, one where she'd had only slightly less to drink than he, it was David who had smoothed it over with the cop with a business card and handshake, David who had called their insurance company and lawyer, David who had worked things out with the other driver so they hadn't even gone to court.

But David couldn't fix what Mark had done, what Mark had become – the killer of his own girlfriend's mother – any more than she could understand it. And now that there's no chance for redemption, Anne wants nothing more than for David to be who he's never been, to tell her what he's feeling instead of thinking. She wants to tell him that she feels cheated by the weather, the hang glider, by so much more. She wants to say that she understands why Theresa would want nothing to do with Mark but not why Theresa would punish them by keeping April away. She wants to ask if he feels the bank cheated him when they sentenced him to wait out retirement as a meager branch manager after the sub-prime market collapsed. She wants to know why he hasn't cried in front of her since they received the phone call from the warden telling them Mark was dead for no other reason than he was at the wrong table in the cafeteria when a fight broke out.

The crash happened on a Saturday in June. Anne was sitting on the veranda sipping coffee with her copy of *As I Lay Dying* in her lap, waiting for Mark to call. She'd meant to open the book immediately, to make good progress that morning so she wouldn't make a fool of herself when the Book Club met on Tuesday, but the truth was she'd been having trouble getting into it. There were too many characters, too much going on. It was like standing in a room amid a torrent of echoing voices, all dimly menacing.

It was the first book she'd read since coming back to the club, and a part of her wished that she'd waited until after they were finished with

Faulkner. But David and the counselor were right. It was time to begin socializing again, to return to the clubs and her volunteer work. After all, hers wasn't the only child who had run into difficulties. Karissa Frey had been expected to graduate as valedictorian of Mark's class before getting pregnant, and now she cut hair for a living when she wasn't down in Asheville doing God-knows-what. Yet that hadn't stopped her mother from being elected to the Friends of the Library board. And while she wouldn't admit it out loud, she was grateful that Mark wasn't in Iraq, even if she still hadn't seen him since the last time he'd been led from the courtroom. There had already been one casualty from Tucker earlier that spring; the local newspaper ran a front-page tribute complete with color photograph of a young man she hadn't recognized smiling in his dress uniform in front of a backdrop of red and white stripes, dead of a mortar attack in Baquba.

Still, Anne couldn't escape the lethargy that set in whenever she thought about fighting through another few pages of incomprehensible Mississippians, so instead she gazed at the trees growing up the face of Killdary. It was something she found herself doing more and more often, just looking at nothing in particular and letting thoughts come in and out of her mind like neighbors waving hello as they walked around the block. She watched the sun make its way above the side, and from where she sat it appeared almost like God's face peeking over the mountain's shoulder. Mark was supposed to call that morning as soon as the phone became free, but Anne had learned while he was still in the treatment ward at Morrison that it could sometimes take hours before that happened, a trend that had continued now that he was at Marion.

"Anne?"

Anne sat up and turned, causing the book to slide off her lap and land on the concrete with a noise that seemed much louder than she thought it should. "Yes?"

"Were you asleep?" David took a few steps towards her but stopped before he was within reach. In his hand was a file folder with the white edges of someone's loan application peeking out. He'd been working a lot more ever since Wachovia had decided to enter the subprime market, spending hours sequestered in the study if he wasn't downtown.

It was an opportunity; Anne understood that. David had survived the merger while simultaneously dealing with Mark's trial, and if the branch turned a profit in this venture it would mean a promotion to the regional headquarters in Winston-Salem at least, possibly even a position at the big headquarters in Charlotte. He'd explained it all – the oak paneled office with a view of the city, the ability to pay off all of Mark's legal expenses at once, a retirement home on the Outer Banks.

"No. Just waiting for Mark to call."

"Well," he said. "I've got to run to the office real quick. I'll have the cell if you need me."

"What about Mark?"

He exhaled in a way that, if he had been five years old Anne would've called a huff. "I've waited long enough," he said. "Besides, I just need to run in for a few things I forgot to bring home yesterday."

She nodded. Arguing wouldn't make any difference. "Be safe," she called as he slid the door closed behind him, the sun's reflection changing the glass from transparent into a solid rectangle of white.

When Anne turned back towards Killdary the hang glider was already in flight, hovering first like a blemish on the face of the sun then swooping towards her, a blue-feathered hawk with flared wings ready to strafe, its path so direct that some nervous impulse told her to duck. It passed with the sound of a flag caught in a gale, so close that she saw the pilot's bearded face just before it vanished beyond the roof of the house. It was an image she would remember, how the man had appeared to be not much older than Mark, his mouth hanging open in what she only could imagine was an expression of pure rapture at finding himself so free and unencumbered.

A moment later the glider returned, now so high the pilot was no more than a pill of onyx suspended underneath, and began ascending directly above her in increasingly wide circles, climbing like it was trying to escape the cage of earth and reach the sun. Anne concentrated on the outline, the blue of the wedge only a shade or two deeper than that of the sky. She was the vortex, the glider a junebug or child's toy airplane that she held by a string, although she couldn't say whether or not she was the anchor or if the glider was going to lift her into the soft cradle of the atmosphere.

The harder she concentrated, the more it became apparent that she was the one affected. She lost sight of the house, the mountain, everything save the glider and its aeriform canvas until even that was gone and she'd relinquished herself fully, allowing every thought or idea and even her own skin to fall away, leaving her blissfully adrift for the first time in years. Her only perception was that the moment was the closest to heaven she would have for a long time, if ever, and she basked in the warm, spreading radiance of being caught between planes, a netherworld without time.

When the glider finally broke the circuit and disappeared around the corner of the house Anne found herself blinking, as if she were at the theater in the moment the curtain falls and the houselights suddenly flip on, dizzy and disoriented by a sky once again populated only by clouds and the blue space between. She waited for the glider to return for as long as she could, the stiffness in her neck and the growing shadows of afternoon seeping back into her consciousness, until eventually she gathered everything, including the Faulkner still lying face-down on the concrete, and went inside.

She was still giddy, but she ate a small lunch and took her second pill of the day anyway, for no other reason than her doctor had directed her to when he wrote out the prescription. She thought about going back out to see if she could catch sight of the glider before it landed at the high school on the northeast side of Killdary. The school's football field had always been the preferred landing strip, the only clear and level piece of ground nearby that wasn't a fairway on the public golf course, and Anne remembered how, in the days gliders sprung off the ramp in such large numbers they seemed to be discarded products of the mountain itself, she would sometimes take Mark over to the stadium to sit in the concrete bleachers and watch them land one by one, Mark clapping each time one touched down like the pilot had performed the greatest magic in the world just for him. If she wasn't waiting for the phone she might've driven over to the school for old times' sake, but instead she lay down on the living room couch where a diamond of sunlight poured through the western window, contenting herself with the idea.

She meant to try again at working her way through the Faulkner while keeping an ear open for the low whine of David's Explorer, but the combination of sun, medicine, and the lingering afterglow of her morning lulled her to sleep, and when she woke up it was to the plastic chirping of the phone's handset on the table beside her.

The caller ID read UNAVAILABLE. Anne pressed Talk and waited with the phone by her side until she knew enough time had passed for her to lift her arm and accept the call without having to hear any more than one or two disjointed words from the cold, mechanized recording. Then there was the requisite thirty seconds of soft hissing broken by sporadic clicks before they were connected. The process had become rote, no more than punching in her PIN at the checkout line.

"Hey." She sat up and placed her feet on the pale hardwood, realizing as she did that she was still alone in the house. There was no sound, no creaking of joists or footsteps across the ceiling, nothing but the white hum from the air conditioning. It was a fact she accepted – David would miss Mark's call.

"Mom?" Mark's voice reached through the static and distant clamor, the muted rumblings of men's voices and occasional loud buzz of what sounded like the scoreboard at Mark's basketball games in high school. "Did I wake you up?"

"No. Well, yes. I must've dozed off waiting for your father to get home."

Anne rubbed her free hand across her face to finish the process of waking. Mark never had much time to talk, though she wasn't sure whether that was due to crowds waiting in line behind him or whatever *introspection*, as he liked to call it, that caused him to prohibit them from visiting. "How are *you*?" she asked.

"Better than in a long time, Mom."

There was something different about his voice, some familiar levity that Anne hadn't heard before in his calls home. It took her a minute to place it, but once she did there was the same beatific expansion in her chest she'd felt watching the hang glider. It was Mark's voice, the Mark she'd raised, the voice that summoned memories of them together in the mornings when Mark was just a child and David had left for work, when they'd lived in a world where their futures were fixedly interwoven and limited only by the maximum amount of magnificence allocated for any two humans. It was a voice that, just like his eyes, exuded potency, vitality, so different from the monotone he'd spoken in since he first went to Morrison.

"You sound good." The words sounded too weak in her ears, too much like a simple platitude. "You sound like yourself, honey," she tried again. It still wasn't right, wasn't enough, but before she could try a third time Mark broke in.

"I've been doing so much reflecting, so much thinking," he said, his speech beginning to rush headlong. "The chaplain here says I've really been making progress, Mom. I'm on Step Eight, making a list of the people I hurt and how I can try and make it up to them."

"I can't tell you how—"

Anne caught herself before she said something trite. She wished that he could see her. Words just weren't adequate. Because it wasn't what Mark was saying that mattered – personally, she was skeptical of twelve-step programs and all the sermonizing that went along with them, though if they helped Mark she was willing to go along – it was the emotion conveyed, and she wanted to reflect that emotion so that somewhere in the middle their echoes would combine and reconcile the awful man Mark had been for those years after dropping out of college with the boy who had so often run around the veranda with his arms outstretched in juvenile imitation of now-forgotten gliders above him, the boy who was and would always be the person she conjured when she thought the words *my son*.

"Honey, I've got to tell you about this hang glider I saw this morning—"

"Mom, there've been hundreds of hang gliders flying off that mountain," Mark interrupted. "I'm sorry. I just don't have much time and I want to tell you that I've started Step Nine. I've made my first amend."

"Okay," she said. It was a delay, not a rejection. Mark had only started sharing these things with her again recently, and, besides, she couldn't help but hope for good news. "How so?" she asked.

"I signed the papers for Theresa's lawyers. I wrote a letter, too, to go with it. Mailed them yesterday."

"The papers for April?"

"Those are the only papers she's sent me, Mom," he said.

And just that quickly it was gone, like she'd swallowed an ice cube, a frozen rock in her throat that spread throughout her body as it melted. The doctor had told her Xanax would "take the edge away" from her black thoughts, but it was more like a speed bump than brakes, slowing the pain to lessen the impact but not stopping it altogether. But in this case it wasn't even a speed bump, more like the difference between being shot in the face and slowly pressed to death.

"Why?" she asked, thinking *Yesterday. Already done, then, no taking it back.*

"What else could I do?" he asked. "I killed her mother—"

"That wasn't you that night, not really. Those drugs …" Anne trailed off, fighting the images she'd purposefully forgotten since the trial. The pictures the police had made, blown-up and pasted on poster board by the District Attorney so that everyone in the courtroom would see the annular pattern of blood on the wall, the gaping red mouth spread across Helen Coffey's chest and know what her son had done.

"It was me," Mark said, the words authoritative but without heat. "And I can't take it back. Only God can truly forgive me, but I can at least give Theresa this."

"But you're her *father*. Not that guy she married."

Anne realized she was crying, the living room dissolving into a whorl of tan and white. She'd been happy only that morning. Where was David?

"Why do you have to be so melodramatic?" he asked.

She sat up. Since when did he use the word "melodramatic?"

"Do you have any idea how long I've spent staring at those papers?" There was a slight pause, and she tried to imagine Mark's face but couldn't read his voice. "Her father? I haven't *seen* her in three years. How can I pretend to be her father?" He sighed. "Besides, I know Mitch Kirby. He's a good man—"

"But what about me?" The shrillness of her voice surprised even Anne. "How could you take her from me?"

"It's not *about* you." Mark's voice had a hiss underneath. "Theresa wants shut of us, all of us … that means you, too."

"You didn't have to give up. I haven't given up."

Anne found herself upstairs in the bedroom, grabbing the picture of April from when she was two where it sat framed on top of the oak dresser alongside Mark's senior portrait and carrying it back down to the living room in a rush, as if to protect the house from any more contamination. It was a futile gesture, she knew, but there had to be some solace in holding the tangible evidence that despite everything, she hadn't given up the expectation that one day she'd be able to fit a new picture into the frame above the one now four years obsolete so that one would never know there had been a gap in the first place.

"What is there to give up? You act like one day this will somehow just go away and I'll be working for Dad at the bank." He paused. "I can't take that shit, I just can't. *That's* why I don't want you to visit. This is hard enough without you trying to make it better …"

Mark kept talking, but it wasn't him she heard anymore. It was David, using the same voice he'd used when Mark came home from Newberry and later when he'd ordered their lawyers not to prepare for an appeal. When had Mark ever sounded like his father? Where was the Mark she knew, the one she'd talked to earlier?

"I don't understand," she said.

"I don't expect you to," he sighed. "But, look. I've kept other people waiting. I should go." There was a pause, then, "I'm writing amends to you, too. You and Dad. I love you, Mom. I'm sorry I'm not better at explaining this to you."

Anne opened her mouth – to say what she wasn't sure – but the leaden thump of heavy plastic ended the call before she found out. She spent the rest of the afternoon watching the patch of sunlight from the window behind her crawl across the floor as all the things that had happened passed through her head indiscriminately until they became a single, solid knot of displaced words and images.

The patch of sunlight had just begun its climb up the far wall when David came through the door, telling a convoluted story about traffic. Anne listened, nodding appropriately when the story seemed to call for it, but it wasn't until the following morning when she saw the front page of the paper that she made the connection. Mark's letters never came.

The Rev. Johannsen is waiting for them when the limo pulls up to the gravesite, standing at the head of the rectangular pit with a Bible held in both hands resting on the slope of his paunch stomach. He walks over once Anne and David have been helped out of the limo by the funeral director and shakes both of their hands with a bowed head.

"Again, I'm so sorry for your loss," he says, repeating the only words that passed between them when they'd met him at Pembroke an hour before. "I can't tell you how special a young man Mark was, how much hope we had for him."

Anne thinks about telling him that it isn't his place to tell her anything about her son or hope or any of the rest, but she decides against it when she sees that his eyes are swollen and pinker than the rest of his face. She'd wanted to hate Johannsen, if for no other reason than he'd seen more of Mark over the past few years than she had, but when he'd walked into the funeral home he had been so opposite of the caricature of an English rector that she'd expected – a gaunt, dour-faced man with sprigs of white hair and a mouth full of Hellfire – that she couldn't. Instead, the minister reminds her of a farmer or country doctor, genial and gentlemanly. And now, as he places one pudgy hand on her elbow to lead her to the grave, she has trouble seeing him as anything other than a lonely old man wearing a clerical collar over an ordinary rib stitched shirt – short and balding with a round Nordic face and lips so pale they practically blend into his pink skin. His voice is so soft she has to strain to hear him above the grinding of the mechanical winch settling the coffin into place above the grave.

"I know you meant a lot to him," she says, taking her position beside David on the near side of the coffin.

Johannsen only nods and places a hand briefly on David's shoulder as he makes his way around the periphery and looks to the funeral director.

"Heavenly Father," he commences in a different voice than he used with Anne before, one so strong and commanding that it seems to be channeling through him. "We have gathered here to mark the end of one life and the beginning of a new, for this man we are committing to this ground now walks alongside You in Your Heavenly Kingdom …"

At first, Anne follows along with her eyes clinched tight against the brightness, but as the cleric continues his litany of imagined rewards her mind begins to wander. She opens her eyes to see Killdary rising in the distance, and she spots the hang glider coasting in front, the red of its wings a sharp contrast to the gray of the trees spreading below and behind, the white expanses of cumulus mottled with blue above and beyond. A breeze sweeps in from the north, brushing against the back of her neck as the minister crescendos to a benediction.

She feels David shift beside her, and when she looks up their eyes meet for just a second. His face contracts in a way that suggests the puckered, browning peal of an overripe orange. It's an expression Anne can't discern before he nods and resumes his stiff-shouldered pose, his hands still clasped together at his midsection. She too looks away, pressing the image of the entire gathering to memory – from Johannsen and his convert being lowered slowly into the ground to the husband at her side to the hang glider floating above the maze of streets and mountains and rows of white marble, strangers all.

Where You Are From

When you were a kid, no more than six, two buildings on Main Street burned within a year of each other. One housed a flower shop and had been painted yellow; the other was already vacant. They weren't side-by-side, but both were less than a block from the town square. The flower shop could be seen from City Hall. Someone – maybe the owners, maybe the city – covered the shattered windows with plywood almost as bright as wheat, and the buildings sat like that for years. As time passed the plywood darkened until each panel was stained to match the streaks of soot that crawled up the buildings' faces like fingers. None of the adults around you seemed to find this abnormal, so neither did you. Like I said, this was when you were a kid, and you had other things to worry about. But – this isn't about you, although you play a part.

The buildings weren't demolished until you were in high school, and the first time you passed the freshly graveled lot you found yourself staring at it, trying to figure out what exactly was missing. Later, the city would build a wall separating the sidewalk from the gravel lots, but that was when the town had more money.

Tucker was a furniture town, prided itself on the fact. The sign on US-321 marking the southern edge of the city limits welcomed visitors to: "Tucker: Furniture Capital of the South." The first factories were built at the end of the nineteenth century following the explosion of logging north of town. The families, the Hills and Dales, that founded those companies have their names everywhere to this day. The civic center is the T.H. Dale Center. The highway (US-321) that splits the town into its eastern and western economic halves is named for T.H.'s brother, Edward. Two parks are named for Jonathan Hill, local corporate titan and one of North Carolina's longest serving Senators, so locals call one "The Walking Park." You still see the names every time they give away furniture on *The Price is Right*, because Hill-Dale Furniture Industries grew and prospered for a century, right here in Tucker.

Your teachers used to point that out to your classes in elementary school. You suppose it was a way of introducing some sort of civic pride. When you were in high school the mantra changed to, "not even the factories will hire you without a GED anymore." Of course, that was in response to the high dropout rate. According to Census Data, only thirteen percent of the citizens of Hopewell County, of which Tucker is the seat, hold a degree from a four-year school. However, a full sixty-eight percent hold at least a high school equivalent. Look on the bright side.

You wonder what they tell the high school students now to scare them.

Just to the north of Tucker are the Blue Ridge Mountains. The Brushy Mountains rise to the south and continue northeastward towards Wilkesboro. Tourists from all over come to these mountains each year for their natural beauty, but growing up among them rendered you immune. Maybe that's common, you aren't sure. Besides, it's not like tourists came to Tucker to see mountains. They went to Boone and Blowing Rock for that, or else they went to Asheville and the southern mountains and didn't even pass through. If tourists stopped in Tucker, it was to do one of two things: eat at one of the burger chains that lined US-321 or shop at one of the discount furniture warehouses south of them.

Maybe "immunity" is the wrong word, because there wasn't a time when you were *un*aware of the mountains. How could you have been? They enshrouded you, like the outer wall of a castle. When you were a small child, this felt protective. Later, when you were older and more things had happened, this felt entrapping. Either way, you remember being amazed on rare family vacations to Myrtle Beach how flat the ocean was. You weren't used to being able to see for miles without first having climbed something. Later, on a Greyhound bus, you would feel the same way about Indiana.

Now that you live in a place that feels only marginally more topographically diverse than Indiana, you find yourself missing the mountains more and more, as if you've suddenly gone colorblind.

You spent the earliest part of your life living in an area of the county called Lord's Creek, and on all four sides of your house you could see the rising Brushies. They were your backdrop, but like a New Yorker your eyes stayed closer to the ground. Your focus was on the alleys, not the spires, and this is what you saw: trailers, scattered satellite dishes, underbrush, dirt lawns with random patches of grass growing like facial hair on a twelve-year-old boy, pieces of metal, aluminum siding, rusted corpses of cars bullet ridden by target practice (in your yard: a '78 Datsun 240Z), old wooden shacks with grayed untreated wood. This is a stereotype of Appalachia, but at the time you didn't know better. There were very few children, and when you encountered one you stared at each other like refugees from two sides of a war zone. If one of you had G.I. Joes or a Nintendo, you would play. But most of the time you were alone.

The mountains encircling Tucker have one relative in town. Killdary Mountain is the highest peak of the Brushies, although saying the "highest peak of the Brushies" is like saying "the least corrupt politician." It doesn't amount to much. Killdary is privately owned, and the owners installed a two-hundred-foot-tall grid of lights on top, right by the fire tower. During Advent a five-pointed star can be seen for miles. During Lent, the lights form a cross. There is a hang glider ramp, but

Where You Are From

after someone died Killdary's owners put up a sign prohibiting anyone from jumping. You missed the gliders once they were gone.

Your father's people – both grandfather and grandmother – were among the first families to settle the area, but your ancestry isn't found on any founders' list. To be a founding family you must first have land, money, or power. There are long sagas attached to why your family never accumulated each, but that's not important. Here's a tidbit just for laughs: your grandmother's grandmother had four children out of wedlock, including your great-grandfather, before she married a tenant farmer. Her name was Mary Magdalene. No shit.

You were born in the last months of Carter's presidency. Your father worked in the sanding room of a plant near the mall, and your mother was the secretary for a textile mill south of town. You remember visiting her there, can still hear the roar of the machines you had to pass to get to the Coke machine, feel the rough hands of the men who would reach down to pat your unprotected head. When the mill closed a few years later to follow the rest of the industry to Mexico for cheaper labor, your mother went back to being a secretary for an accountant. That's foreshadowing, but somehow none of the adults in your life caught it.

In town, you stayed with your paternal grandparents while your parents worked. Your grandfather loved to walk, and he would take you with him to the neighborhood school, where he taught you your alphabet from the letters painted on the sides of the school buses. That is also where he taught you to ride a bike when you were nine. You remember your grandfather once pointing out a crackpipe fashioned out of a Sun-Drop bottle and dropped near a swing. He warned you never to let him catch you playing with "one of those things," which was good advice because you saw a lot, and many looked pretty neat. He didn't have to tell you not to play with the needles; you were afraid of them already. In your twenties you would relate this story to a young man who responded, "Yeah, addiction is terrible." You had to explain that your grandfather was more worried about you catching hepatitis. Remember, this wasn't considered a poor neighborhood, it was just what your side of Tucker was like. If the adults didn't seem concerned, why should you?

At home, your parents, like most people's your age, got divorced. The pattern: they would fight for two weeks then your father would disappear for a few months. This went on for years and affected you in all the expected ways. You blamed yourself, and you became sullen and withdrawn. When I said earlier that you had other things to worry about besides those burnt-out buildings downtown, this is what I meant. Besides, it wasn't like those two were the only burnt buildings in Tucker. Hell, they weren't even the only ones downtown. The furniture industry had been in a slump since the mid-70s, and, by extension, so had Tucker. When you were old enough to take walks without your grandfather, you would go downtown and watch bums bathe in the fountain across the street from the courthouse. More buildings were demolished, and those that weren't had their windows boarded up because there was enough broken glass on the streets as it was. In the summer the shards shone like tiny mirrors. During the winter they hid in snowballs. You tasted blood for the first time that way.

Sometimes all this sounds bad or pitiable, and you wish you'd been raised in Upper Creek. That's on the east side of town, and there they have sidewalks without crackpipes and day-glow lawns. They also have cul-de-sacs. But you didn't live there; you lived on the west side of town and this is what you saw. You're not complaining. After all, life isn't a fairy tale, and things were much worse for a large, large number of people. Hell, we're not talking about Detroit.

And, things were about to get better. The 1990s were great years for the furniture industry, and, by extension, Tucker. The local newspaper predicted years of gains in the market. At one point they reported orders were up over seventy-five percent. The county's unemployment dropped to under five percent for the first time in years, then it fell below three, then two percent. After NAFTA was passed Hispanic immigrants flooded the town, and at the time no one minded because there was plenty of work to go around. This is when the city got the money to demolish those burnt shells on Main Street. You saw fewer bums, fewer pipes. There didn't even seem to be as much glass. Economically, downtown was as dead as it had been, but at least trees were planted.

During these years, your father was promoted at the plant, reappeared, and bought a house in your grandparents' neighborhood. You saw him regularly for the first time in over five years. The local newspaper began running the first articles about "economic diversification," but with such a low unemployment rate and relatively uneducated workforce it was nearly impossible to lure new industries. Not that Tucker needed them. Remember, the industry was booming, and almost every adult you knew either worked in the plants or worked because of the plants. Your mother was still at the accountant's, but your father worked in the plants and so had both grandfathers. You were supposed to work there, too, but you went to college with your parents' blessing and more debt than either of them made in a year.

Once you moved away, you immediately realized how provincial you were. You adopted a "better" manner of speaking as best you could. Got rid of your redneck accent. You cut your hair and beard. You still loved your family, but you decided you belonged to a different world. Shame and guilt fed each other. In trying to escape the clichés of your upbringing you became another one. You got above your raising.

Wouldn't that make for a nice ending? One to make Horatio Alger proud? Except it wouldn't be true. But, then again, only you know how much of this is true and how much isn't. Also, remember that foreshadowing?

Here's what happened after you left. Furniture followed you, but it went to China instead of Boone. In the year 2001 alone, Hopewell County's unemployment went from 1.9% to 11%. By 2003 it was up to 13.6%. Even during the worst stretches, unemployment in Tucker had never been above 8.5%. And while there had been layoffs in the past, there had never been closures. Factories became empty shells; the machines were stripped for parts. The tax base plummeted, and the city cut back on services such as police patrols and Health Department staff. The recycling program was cut altogether. Here's another set of numbers: At its height, Hill-Dale Furniture, and all its subsidiary companies such as Hopewell Chair, employed 8,000 people within the incorporated boundary of Tucker alone. Now the company website lists 2,400 workers nationwide. Even before the housing bubble popped for the rest of the country, foreclosures in Tucker skyrocketed. In a single week during the spring of 2005, the local newspaper published over four hundred notices. On the pages that came before were articles about the rising number of methamphetamine arrests in the area. Apparently, people wanted to do more with their newfound time.

Your father was one of the first to lose his job. In the summer of 2002, he'd been with the company for nineteen and a half years, and just a few years prior he'd been promoted. Therefore, he was a bigger financial liability to the company. He is still unemployed to this day, and lives in your grandparents' basement, in the same room he'd had as a child. Your mother's job lasted a year beyond your father's, but, in the end, the accounting firm she'd worked for closed as well. The majority of their clients were small businesses – restaurants and car mechanics –

and without much income to tax, those businesses found that they didn't need an accountant to prepare them. Your mother's car was taken first, towed in the middle of the night to a lot in Rhyne where she recovered her belongings the next day. Her house, the one in Lord's Creek, became the bank's a month later. Eventually she would file bankruptcy, and you would learn a trick of the law: Even after property is repossessed, the borrower still owes the lender the remaining balance of the original loan, minus recuperation. Neat trick, huh?

Even through your expatriation you took these events hard. Now the shame and guilt you felt had more to do with trying to shed where you came from. You readopted your native accent. You did genealogy projects. You went back to Tucker for Christmas and photographed the pipes and syringes that were once again dotting the streets and sidewalks.

That's the sad ending, the one where everyone realizes the true cost of words like *globalization* and Tucker fades into memory like a rust belt ghost town. But just as life isn't a fairy tale, it isn't a Bruce Springsteen song, either.

Here's what happened next. The civic leaders of Tucker – the very same ones who had sat in boardrooms and made decisions about plant relocations, had scouted locales as far away as Canton, People's Republic of China – remembered that Tucker was in the Blue Ridge Mountains. They changed the sign at the edge of the city limits to read: "Tucker: Where the High Country Begins." They lured real estate developers to buy hundreds of acres north of town in the hopes of siphoning some of the retirement home market away from Spruce Pine and Linville. Downtown, they launched a revitalization campaign, enticing the town's first coffeeshop (that wasn't a Waffle House) and bookstore (that didn't only sell Bibles). Three new restaurants opened.

However, other than a few low-end service sector jobs and

seasonal construction work, this didn't lead to a return of jobs. So, the local community college launched new programs in order to lure technology companies, and the city threw in tax breaks for any willing to make the leap. To compensate, they raised property taxes for homeowners 22.2% just before the sub-prime mortgage market collapsed in 2007. Those two factors haven't helped the retirement-home market much, to say the least, although developers are still bulldozing forests as I write this. It didn't help those still hanging on to their homes, either.

So, what happened next? Where is the neat little package, the sense of resolution? Well, we've already established that life is neither a fairy tale or Springsteen song, but what hasn't been said is that there are no real endings at all. Tucker remains and will continue to do so barring natural or nuclear catastrophe. And, the people remain. Your father still sits with your grandmother all day trying to think of a legitimate way to earn money. Your mother has a new job, again as a secretary, and she lives with her boyfriend in a trailer outside of Rhyne. You somehow found your way into graduate school.

Before you went, your mother asked you not to forget them.

Acknowledgments

These works have appeared in slightly different forms in the following:

Monongahela Review: "It Felt Like Spring"
The Saturday Evening Post: "Strangers All" published as "Falcons of Killdary"

First, thank you to the editors at Redhawk Publications who saw value in this manuscript and helped bring it to the light of day. I would also like to thank all the writers, mentors, institutions, and teachers who taught me love for the craft and aided in my own development: B.C. Crawford, Jade Huynh, Joseph Bathanti, Wilton Barnhardt, John Kessel, Jill McCorkle, Tony Earley, Eric Roe, Shailen Mishra, the NC State MFA Program, the Sewanee Writers Conference, and so many more.

To my employers and colleagues throughout the years at Kansas State University, especially the Department of English and K-State First; at Catawba Valley Community College; at Hickory Career and Arts Magnet High School; and now at Greensboro College Middle College: this work would not be possible without your steadfast (and often undeserved) support. Poet and scholar Dr. Rand Brandes's generosity in welcoming me to the wonderful Hickory creative community is a debt that cannot be repaid. I have felt honored and just a bit of impostor syndrome working alongside you all.

To my students past and present, you inspire me every day. Thank you to Dustin Ring, Anastasia Turley, and especially Paul Funderburk; y'all literally (in the original sense) saved my life. I love you. Thank you. I would also like to thank my family: my late father, Douglas Nelson; my mother and stepfather Karen and Randy McClough; brothers Randy Jr.

Where You Are From

(and family) and Nathan McClough; my sister Ginny Lilly and family; and all the Nelsons and Allisons past, present, and future.

Thank you to my friends who have seen me through the years and decades – Lenoir, Triangle, Asheville, Manhattan, and in between. I love you all. If anyone thinks they see themselves in any of these stories, they don't.

And, last but certainly not least, I would like to thank Allyson for giving me a reason. You have no idea the depth of my love nor expanse of my gratitude.

About The Author

Christopher L. Nelson is a native of Lenoir, NC who received his MFA from North Carolina State University. After teaching at a midwestern university for several years, he currently lives between Greensboro and Western North Carolina with his partner, two cats, and a dog.

Made in the USA
Middletown, DE
08 February 2025